Stalking the Hydra

A case of mistaken identity leads to a hunt for vengeance by the Author of Hurricane Road.

A novel by:
Roger C Horton

Second, Edition
Copyright(C)2020 by Roger C Horton
All rights reserved by the author

ISBN 978-0-9906808-1-9
Cover illustration: Roger Horton

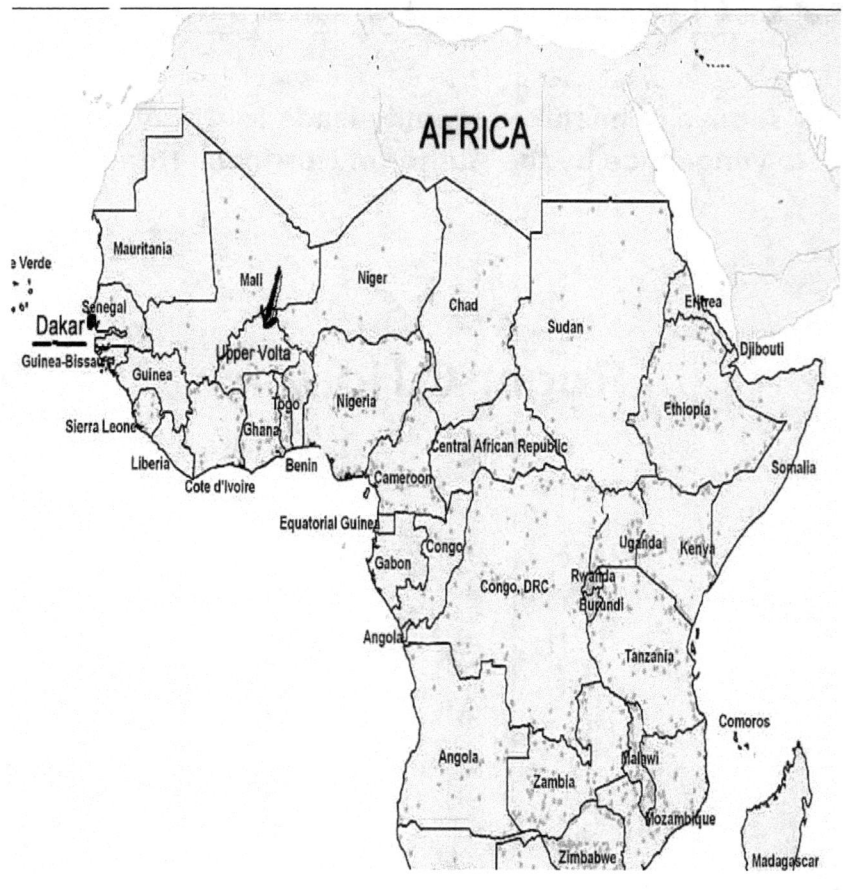

Introduction

A case of mistaken identity as the target of an assassination, begins a deadly two-way game of cat and mouse across three continents. Driven by anger and the need for vengeance an ex-special forces sergeant, stalks members of a powerful multinational cartel, even as he is hunted by it's Chief of Security. The novel is played out in mid-1970's in Africa the US and Europe, in a swirl of non-stop and lethal action.

Author's Note:

This novel was written after time spent in Central Africa in the mid-1970s. Although the story is a total work of fiction, it holds a lot of observation of the general trends. Over the years, it has been surprising though, to watch how some of the events alluded to actually came to pass. Of course, all names have been changed to protect the guilty.

Stalking the Hydra

**Other Books by
Roger C Horton**

1

--An unfortunate error

We are but pieces in a game he plays
Upon a checkerboard of nights and days,
One by one, he moves, he checks, he slays.

-Rubaiyat, of Omar Khayyam

On the northern slopes the month was June, the season of rain, yet a dry yellow wind still swept the land. Sandstorms roiled across the plateau, driving nomads and farming people alike, south in hope of finding food and water. In this seventh year of drought even the pride of the nomadic Taureg's had buckled -- they too stumbled into the relief centers seeking food that they were often too debilitated to benefit from.

Jerry Carlton had spent three days with a truckload of food, lurching in and out of ditches over ruts; grinding up gradients. Crater pocked, the unpaved road north from Dedougou was rock hard in places, covered with drifting sand in others. On the return trip he had carried fifty Mosi and Bobo tribesmen to Dedougou's refugee center. They had climbed down regularly to help drag the big truck up grades, through sand, and even then, the African road had battered the machine, nearly to junk.

The brown, red sun had long been replaced by a dull half-moon when Jerry arrived in Dedougou. As an official of the UN Food and Agriculture organization in the country of Upper Volta, he made intermittent trips, to judge conditions in the various northern villages. Their situations were all becoming the same, awful! He had been with the F.A.O. since July of '72, five long years.

The F. O. A. 's mission, was to help countries modernize or develop agriculture, while improving the diets of their people. That was the plan but the dry sub Saharan winds were blowing away what little soil had existed to begin with in the Central African country. People starved by the thousands, and though relief food was available, it seemed always to be late, misdirected, or not enough. People ignorant of international boundaries poured out of Mali and Niger to seek succor and they added to the problem. F.A.O. sponsored the building of wind walls to retain soil, the damming of creeks, planting of trees and cover crops, but the most ignorant tribesman knew that only with steady rain would there be relief. Organizations toiled, people suffered, and little concrete success was achieved. Jerry was sick with the frustration of it.

He had been a Planning Director in West Africa for the last two years, rising rapidly in lower ranks of the UN bureaucracy as much from his seeming ability to repeal personal disease and injury, as to owning skill as an administrator. He was not a big man, less than six feet, but not small either, he was muscular and leather tough, from a decade of exposure to the elements of nature. Durable as he was, the conditions he was operating under, were not what he had in mind when he joined the UN organization. The endless problems of his job were what occupied his mind as he entered his bungalow, calling to his wife. He was startled by a man rising to introduce himself.

"Monsieur Carlton?" the slender silhouette questioned.

"Oui," Jerry answered, allowing the conversation to continue in French.

"Allow me to introduce myself, Mr. Carlton; Louis Renard. I am a journalist and have hoped that you could perhaps help me in a small way. Your wife has retired but kindly allowed me to wait for you."

Stepping forward to shake his hand, Jerry said, "A pleasure." The man emitted an acid nervous odor that belied his calm manner, and Jerry continued, "If its information on F.A.O., Mr. Renard, I'd much rather we meet at the office in the morning. I've made a somewhat arduous trip during the last few days and I've been looking forward to a shower, and some rest."

"I realize this, Mr. Carlton, but time is of the essence for me. At the moment, I find myself in an exposed position -- in relation to certain political elements. You understand how it is. Ah! Please, do you mind if we continue in the dark?"

Jerry had been fumbling for a light switch and stopped out of courtesy. He was dead tired yet the bizarre approach of the Frenchman -- his paranoia, had drawn on his curiosity. "May I get you a drink, that is, if I can find something in the dark? Beer all right with you?"

"Yes, thank you," Renard said sitting down again, listening in silence to Jerry fumbling in the kitchen. A large insect of some sort crawled up his leg, and swatting it off, he stomped on it.

"Now, what is it that you wish to know, Mr. Renard?" Jerry asked, as he returned moments later with a pair of chilled cans.

Taking a sip Renard smiled and began, "I have by accident uncovered a nest of scorpions," he said almost fearfully, not speaking of the insect he had just crushed. "It was in the Western Sudan that I first turned over the rock, but at that time I did not realize the full significance, the dimensions of what I now suspect. Only six weeks ago my daughter, my son, and myself began to research and interview for an article I wished to do on the various actions that have been taken to combat famine by the countries of the drought belt: effects, economics, so forth. As I said, the original key piece of information was pure chance, but it has led me to similar discoveries in eight other countries now; and not only countries in the drought region. Now the question. You were, I'm told, with F.A.O. in Dabuta three years ago when General Zwazi took power."

"Yes," Jerry answered, now almost sure of a hint of suppressed fear in Renard's voice.

"How well did things go before the coup, I mean shipments, services, your impressions of the government, industrial growth, state of affairs?"

Jerry leaned back and thought to himself for a moment. In June of '72 he had just completed the jamming of three years of graduate work into two years on a quarterly system: agricultural courses, administration, transportation, even a spattering of African History, and political science. He had begun his work with the United Nations Agency with the fever of a missionary among heathens. His experiences in Indochina had left him with a desire to do something positive to help people. Large numbers of people, children particularly for they seemed always to take the brunt of calamity. He looked at Renard and began to speak of Dabuta.

"Things were at least stable when I arrived in Brazzaville in '72," he said. "Ani Petumba was president, and the government was making some progress."

"F.A.O. was involved in a large tabling and irrigation project, as well as advising the government on modernization and expansion of the lumber industry. Some zinc deposits of commercial value had been discovered, and I believe British Petroleum had a survey going for oil."

"I'd been there for about four months when things began to go wrong, it was plain screwy. Machinery broke down and spare parts that arrived were the wrong ones. Local industries seemed to run into marketing problems. Loans arranged in Europe, fell through and to top things off, a ship taking a lumber cargo caught fire and half the port along with grain warehouses burned with it. After the fire they attempted to move it to sea, but it capsized and sank in the main channel. There had been a poor crop that year in the highlands and with no food available things became unstable. Rival political parties began to agitate. There were a large number of murders, and finally riots, when tribesmen swelling into the cities in search of work and food, clashed with police."

"The entire system became a shamble within six months. Some UN people were killed along with a few European businessmen. Power, communication, everything came to a halt, and then General Zwangi stepped in with a surprise private army. Of course, you know the rest. End of civilian rule, political executions, torture, etc. Everyone that could, ran for the hills. Roads were a death trap, I walked out myself, and from what I've witnessed that's the normal cycle for ex-colonial African countries," Jerry added.

"Tell me one more thing," Renard said, his chin resting on the palm of his hand as he spoke. "Do you believe that the events leading up to the disorder and eventual take-over were accidental or manufactured; did you gain an impression of something amiss; sabotage, shall we say?"

"Mr. Renard, perhaps I am somehow lacking in perceptiveness, but it seemed to me more bad luck and bungling than conspiracy. Of course, my exposure was limited to one small rural area for the greater part of my stay in Dabuta. From what I'm familiar with, to have sabotage on that scale it would have required a subtle organization over time and a vast area. My experience--it's usually in the nature of things to go wrong on their own here."

"Understandable, but it is an organized and quite subtle force that I am speaking of," Renard sighed.

Jerry looked at his watch it was past midnight. "It's very late, Mr. Renard, and I have work tomorrow and a long drive to Bobo Dioulasso," Jerry said standing. "If you want to stay, you're welcome to the hammock for the night. "I'm sorry I couldn't be of more help to you."

"Ha!" said Renard. "I accept your invitation and offer you one. Henri and Nicole managed to catch a lift directly to Dakar this afternoon. A private aircraft belonging to an acquaintance. My jeep is air-conditioned and if you don't mind the company? We three did have reservations from Bobo Dioulasso to Dakar, so I'm going there myself tomorrow."

"Thank you, but my wife is going to be traveling with me," Jerry said, beginning to feel somewhat irritated with the man.

"She is even more welcome, of course, but get your bath and rest. Tomorrow, whatever," Renard said spreading the hammock to climb in. Succeeding in the maneuver, he folded his hands behind his head and called, "Good night, Monsieur."

***

It was in the vicinity of seven a.m. when voices and the clatter of dishes woke Jerry. He recognized Connie's voice, but could not place the man until he remembered Renard. Climbing out of bed, he stumbled to the bath, splashed water on his face and decided he needed a shave. A few moments later, Jerry emerged looking as keen as he felt, and slapped his wife on the rump as he entered the kitchen.

"Hey, that's no way to treat a lady," she protested, swiping him with a greasy spatula.

"Okay, peace," he yelled, ducking back with a laugh.

"Good morning, Monsieur, you appear to have rested well," Renard said from the adjoining room.

"Yes, very well."

Renard continued, "and what of the transport, have you decided to accept?"

"Your damned right we accept air conditioning," Connie said, before Jerry could open his mouth.

"Looks like it's decided, Renard," Jerry said, half smiling.

They took time with breakfast, Connie and Renard carrying the bulk of the conversation. She had finished her packing early and intended to surprise him with breakfast, but finding Renard there, she had been surprised herself.

Jerry's wife was the kind of woman one would picture tramping through backward places in the employ of humanity. She was tall, possessing a certain buoyancy, a handsome rather than pretty woman, with flaxen hair, and a strong proportionate body. She moved with a power, rather than grace. She had studied Veterinary Medicine in California, and spent a year in the Peace Corps before joining F.A.O. She was intelligent, and generous, moreover she was Jerry's match. The trip south to Bobo Dioulasso was to make connections for a flight to Connie's hometown in Oregon. Jerry was planning a week of vacationing but she was three months into her first pregnancy and would stay in Oregon during the remainder of the year. She didn't like the idea of being separated from her husband but on the other hand, she preferred the security of her parents' home during her first pregnancy.

It was nearly eleven a.m. when Jerry finished going over papers with his assistant and climbed into Renard's jeep. The dirt and gravel road ran south along the Volta River. They passed groups of refugees traveling south, water bags slung under donkeys. The bones of animals and trees alike decorated the barren sands for the first ninety miles. The land became greener as the road neared the river again and ran along the rim of the basin. Connie had gotten Renard to talking about his work and family. Some of the past triumphs of his career, but he avoided any direct comment on his present project.

"Wait a while," he said, "and you may read of it in detail. I have fitted only a few pieces of the thing together, but enough to understand the danger of what I know. This is why I sought to get Henri and Nicole out at the first opportunity, and why I waste no time in following. Once in

Europe, I will investigate more discreetly," Renard promised somberly.

"How is it that your family and you work together, Louis?" Connie asked.

"Not so really," Renard said. "Nicole is a natural linguist; very little study is required by her to command a language, but her passion is for everything. She could not hold a degree in everything, so she chose linguistics and journalism while dabbling in everything. Everything includes my projects of course."

A couple of vehicles seemed to be stopped a half-mile ahead. Renard noted it and continued to talk. "Now Henri came along for the experience. A very romantic young man, yet his profession is engineering. He had just finished his military career and was not yet ready for a serious endeavor of his own, so he chose to join me."

They were rapidly approaching the curve now and Renard began to slow. It looked like a very serious accident. A truck had overturned and two camels lay dead where the truck had plowed into them. The other truck had only stopped to assist but was blocking the road. Two or three men lay on the ground in apparent pain.

"My God," Connie said as the jeep pulled up. "Let's see if we can help."

"Those fools only know one speed," Renard muttered climbing from the jeep.

Jerry sitting in the back began to climb out behind Connie. One of the several shouting natives, who had rushed milling around the jeep when they pulled up, suddenly brought a knobby stick from beneath his robe, swinging it in a rapid air-slicing arch toward Jerry's head. Jerry caught the motion from the corner of his eye and tried to dive forward twisting under the blow. Even though it was a glancing blow, a brilliant pain exploded behind his eyes, sending a tingling sensation through his body as he plowed limply into the gravel. He could hear grunts, shuffling and Connie's scream, followed by dull thudding sounds. Hands lifted him roughly, thrusting him back into the rear of the jeep. His vision began to clear, but he couldn't seem to control his body. Renard and Connie were being jammed unconscious into the front. Connie's head was tilted back over the seat; a raw graze marred her forehead and blood trickled from her nose; Renard was slumped forward against the wheel. One of the natives shoved him roughly sideways and turned the wheel, yelling an order. Jerry's mind reeled. He couldn't believe what was happening. Under the weight of the blacks, the jeep was beginning to roll. It bumped off the edge of the road. The front wheels lost contact and the undercarriage crashed down onto the rocky edge of the canyon. The men began to chant in rhythm as they rocked the jeep forward. Feeling was beginning to come back into his fingers and he found himself clutching the seat as the front wheels slammed down. There was a sound of metal grinding against rock and the jeep began sliding, rolling down the steep slope toward the Volta River. Two thirds of the way down the forty-five-degree slope, the jeep rammed a boulder, pitch poling ten feet into the air to land on its back bumper; bounced back on its wheels, slid sideways and rolled into the river.

The collision with the boulder flung Jerry against the back of the front seat, then up into the roof as the jeep flipped. The impact of landing rear first sprung the back doors and catapulted him through them.

The air exploded from his lungs as he hit the ground. Squirming and crawling to his knees in an effort to regain his breath, he saw the jeep disappear in a mass of foam. He moved toward the river crawling at first, then in a crouched run as his breath came back. There were excited shouts from the road, but he paid no attention.

His mind writhed in vicarious pain and horror for the woman now trapped below the surface of the swift river. Diving off the bank at a run he hit the water where the jeep had disappeared. A split second later, the current bashed him against the jeep. Holding tight, he felt for the door only to realize the top had been smashed level with the body. Bracing his feet, he heaved on the door with all his strength, but couldn't budge it. His lungs ached, but he knew he'd lose the jeep if he surfaced to take a breath.

He moved around the front feeling his way in the muddy water, the current tearing at him. "Maybe an opening in the windshield," he thought. His hand came in contact with something soft, Connie's shoulder; he could feel her hair sweeping against his arm. Clutching her arm, he pulled; he reached to where she was caught and groaned inwardly. She had been crushed between hood and roof.

Black spots and flashes were passing before his eyes as he let go, kicking for the surface. He treaded water for a few seconds getting his breath, letting the Volta carry him downstream. His body quivered slightly as he swam, but his eyes burned.

Four men had stumbled down the steep embankment to the river, two were armed and one of them was white. They had seen him and begun to pursue along the bank. The black stopped, aiming to shoot, but the white man slapped the barrel down, sending the bullet singing off the rock bank. "They want an accident," Jerry told himself, ducking underwater as old reflexes and training began to control the conscious part of his mind. "He would give them an accident; he would give them one they hadn't planned on."

Jerry popped to the surface once more, took a deep breath; then flailing his arms as if floundering, he allowed himself to sink back beneath the surface. He swam strongly toward the bank hoping to reach shore where the river had cut under the rock, forming a shallow ledge.

The swift water slammed him into a boulder and he bumped his head when he came up for air. When he tilted his head back to take advantage of the four inches of breathing space, he discovered that his neck hurt. He was sore in several places but knew he had escaped serious injury. The original blow had glanced off his head landing solidly at the left back side of his neck, stunning and momentarily paralyzing him, but not crippling. He could run or fight unhampered.

The hunters passed overhead, no sound, just bits of sand and rock splashing into the water. Searching out one hand hold at a time, Jerry began pulling himself upstream. They were about one hundred and fifty meters downstream when Jerry began to crawl toward the road. They had stopped and the white man was giving orders. The two blacks without rifles jumped into the water, one working upstream, one downstream along the bank. The white man moved downstream covering his man, the black man upstream covering his.

"Shit," Jerry said under his breath, they'd spot the wet area where he'd left the water. "No matter," he thought; "if I can't take a single man I'll deserve what I get." He began crawling parallel to the river, toward the hunters and a limestone shelf. He reached the shelf while they were still fifty meters away and he crouched, waiting.

The native was quick, he had to give him that much. He spun, jabbing the rifle toward Jerry's stomach. Without a second's hesitation, Jerry grabbed the barrel with one hand jerking it past his stomach, pulling the man forward off balance. His left hand sunk into the black man's throat at the base of the larynx, right hand releasing the rifle, stiff armed, palm up connecting at the base of the nose. The native dropped like a rock.

Jerry looked up and downstream, but no one had spotted him. He took the man's rifle and knife, placed the latter behind the black's ear and shoved it in twisting. Then crouching he began to run upstream toward the ledge. He spotted the top of the second African's hair as he waded against the current, machete held above his head. Jerry left the rifle, crawling out onto the ledge to intercept the hunter. He poised himself, grabbing a handful of kinky hair and snatched the head backward.

His knife entered the man's right eye, sinking to the hilt, and snapping off as the body convulsed.

Without any sign of emotion, he turned, retrieved the rifle, and began working his way up the cliff to the road. The rifle was an Enfield 303. It carried five rounds, so he had at least four. He slipped the magazine out and counted to make sure. Possibly he could take the truck. He didn't like the idea of being pursued by expert trackers, with only four rounds. He would live only so long as he stayed on the offensive and made no mistakes. One of the first things he'd learned at S.F. school had been the proper times to run attack and hide. "Hiding was out of the question, and running offered small chance of escape," he concluded. "His advantage lay in complete unawareness, on the enemy's part, of his condition or whereabouts."

Jerry spotted one more rifle. It was propped alongside the driver's seat of the big Mercedes truck. He looked to his rear once more and advanced to within fifty feet of the truck. It was perpendicular to the other truck which lay broadside in the road. The earth had been scraped from under the wheels and the body jacked up so it would tend to right itself rather than slide sideways. The head man climbed into the cab revving the engine, the truck moved slowly against the chains as the other five natives strained pushing from behind the overturned truck. Jerry pulled the trigger shattering the windshield as well as the driver's skull. The truck leaped against the chains breaking one and stalling.

In an instant, Jerry was up and running, working the bolt. As the first Samo appeared from behind the truck,

Jerry snapped a shot at the man's chest, but the bullet caught him in the groin. He began to roll screaming across the road.

Jerry worked the bolt again, "two rounds gone," he thought, and leaping onto the running board of the truck, he clutched the other rifle. A rapid glance and he dashed for higher ground above the road, working quickly to his left, above and behind the truck.

Four men were huddled against the body of the truck. He took deliberate aim hitting the farthest man first. Three heads jerked toward the newly dead body and Jerry shot a second man through the neck. In their terror the other two bolted directly for him and died before they realized their mistake.

He jacked the last round out of the one Enfield; took the magazine from the other; he slid the bullet in and replaced the magazine. "Three rounds," he thought. This had been slaughter; now would come the difficult part. He had considered taking the truck immediately, but odds were in favor of a rifle being trained on the truck. Now it would be a waiting game. Jerry rubbed dirt into his face, sand in his hair and shoved some weeds in his collar and shirt pockets. He positioned himself where a patch of shrub grew from a crevice. Nearly invisible from below, he lay perfectly still, waiting and wondering what had just happened to his life

2

"Overconfidence is never so great an error as lack of awareness. While the first may lose you the battle the second can lose the campaign.
Brig. Gen. A. B. Davis

Karl Van Riebeeck was not a stupid man. He had however just done a stupid thing but he did not intend to follow the first stupid thing with a second. The emotional mixture of pride and relief he had experienced as the Renard's jeep had crashed downhill into the river had been replaced by a mild irritation at the sight of his son Henri's, stumbling dash to the river. "A minor problem to be taken care of while the truck was being righted," he had thought. They would catch the injured man and Doube' would hold him underwater until he drowned. The current had been strong though, which had necessitated pursuit and then Renard had disappeared. Van Riebeeck was sure he was hiding on the east bank. They had watched and no sign of Henri or his body had showed in the wide shallows a short distance down river. He and Doube' would watch, and the two Samo would flush the man out. This is where he'd blundered. He'd made the assumption of injury and also failed to take into consideration, the possibility that even an engineering officer in the French Army might possibly have acquired combat skills worth consideration.

"Paaft," he muttered under his breath. "Complacency is the greatest danger."

Van Riebeeck was beginning to feel a bit uneasy even before the Soma's body had floated past. The shooting began only a moment after he had discovered Doube's body. The eyes and nose had been filled with blood telling him that the big man had been taken from the front; taken without a weapon, quickly, and in relative silence. Van Riebeeck could not imagine this being done to Doube'. The man was strong and quick as a cat. Doube' had made his living doing this sort of thing to other people.

The sound of the rifle had sent Van Riebeeck diving for cover, but the second shot brought him out again. "The man is between two forces and had but two rounds left," he told himself. He began to climb toward the road through an area with good cover. Fifty seconds later the last of four evenly spaced shots echoed down the canyon, and he froze. Karl had been seven years an officer in the Dutch East Indies. One learned things, like discerning the meaning of the sound of a weapon. When in combat, one learned or one died. All four rounds had the same sharp crack and had been evenly and expertly spaced. Renard had the other rifle and the Kaffirs were dead. He knew that as well as if he had been standing there watching the man. "He would go for the truck now," Van Riebeeck told his self, beginning to scramble up the slope at his best speed.

At the top he threw himself flat. He sighted on the truck's cab from beneath a log, whispering to his Somo to keep back. Ten minutes later he admitted to underestimating the young man again. With the admission came a certain amount of respect for Renard. It was a standoff. Each wanted the truck and the other dead. Before long, other traffic would happen along creating an entirely untenable situation. As in chess, one must know when to retain a defensive posture in order to organize a more successful attack.

He shifted his bulk and eased backward; he crouched and began picking his way back into the scrub. When he judged himself at a safe distance, he lit a cigarette and drew on it, curses bugs, jungle, desert, and all ignorant savages. He would avoid Africa, henceforth, he promised himself this for the thousandth time. It took him over five hours to walk the twenty miles into Bobo Dioulasso. His feet ached and his legs were numb, but he had set his best pace, except for intermittent stops to guard against possible pursuit. He would take no more chances. A mile from the city, he swung abruptly putting a bullet into the Somo's forehead. He then wiped the weapon down with his shirttail and dropped in next to the body. With the last trace of his culpability attended to, he made his way into town.

Young Renard would depart by plane, and Van Riebeeck would see to it that he was intercepted at the airport. If missed here, he would be killed in Dakar. Arriving at his hotel, he immediately made five calls; the first was to arrange for the acquisition and distribution of photographs of Renard. This done he made his sixth call.

"Good evening sir," he said into the phone.

"The breech?" a precise voice three thousand miles away questioned.

"The breech has been filled with one exception," Van Riebeeck said.

"Be more definite."

"Two thirds filled Sir; the younger third sealed in this locality. I'll keep you informed of any developments and send details later."

"I'm displeased with the delay," the precise voice said. "Ineptitude is intolerable; a security director is not allowed missteps."

"I have taken this problem over personally, Sir, to avoid further mistakes. I might add that the problem didn't originate with security and if there is a delay it will be minor. Very minor."

"As you have pointed out so astutely, the trouble did develop elsewhere," the voice soothed. "So, I should anticipate no setbacks or delays now that you have assured me, Herr Van Riebeeck. I will notify the group that you will not disappoint them."

The line went dead; but within seconds Van Riebeeck was making the first of another series of calls. At all cost Henri Renard must die and soon. Few who had ever dealt with the Dutchman had seen him stressed. Those capable of recognizing the signs would have seen them twice today. Karl Van Riebeeck did not intend tomorrow evens to proceed in a similar manor.

***

A half dozen vultures arrived twenty minutes after Jerry had taken his position. A group of Lobi tribesmen were the next to appear. They tore articles of clothing and jewelry from the bodies, and a hydraulic jack from the trunk. When one of them spotted dust approaching from the south, the band bolted into the bushes.

The dust was from a battered bus, which had turned around and headed back toward Bobo Dioulasso after making the discovery. There were three more vehicles and a dozen natives milling around when police and a contingent of soldiers arrived fifty minutes later.

By this time Jerry had pulled back a couple of hundred yards. He began to move north at an easy run when the troops arrived. He had had time for circumspect examination of the previous twenty-four hours, on which he now based several decisions.

He concluded that someone, probably the man he had alternately fled and stalked during the last hour, had made a mistake. He had expected a jeep heading south on this road with three Europeans: male late forties, a male and female early to mid-twenties. There are only a few thousand Europeans in the whole of Upper Volta. It was easy to surmise that the assassins had expected three Renard's and so had made an understandable error in assuming they had intercepted three Renard's. From an impartial point of view, the slip was almost excusable. A man, who has witnessed the ruthless, brutal murder of the woman he loves, cannot be described as impartial though, not in the most remote understanding of the word.

The eight men Jerry had exterminated had not begun to stem the burning rage in him. Waiting behind the rifle sights, he had tempered the emotion, cooled it, given it direction. Something Louis Renard had learned had become a threat and somewhere that threat had been felt. Whether the threat had been poised against man or empire, Jerry did not know, only that with the casual power of the omnipotent, something had reached out from far away and killed his wife.

The natives here had been mere fingers; the white man the hand; he would find the head, the heart, and repay in kind. He had the motivation, but more important, the resources. At first there would be a need for haste in order to expose his opponents. Later he could plan carefully. It was nearly dark when the last truck pulled out heading for the city. He placed the Enfield on the riverbank with his clothes and started into the water diving to the jeep. He pulled himself into the rear of the wreck feeling for baggage and swam into Renard's mangled face.

Choking and strangling he fought his way back to the surface. It was another ten minutes before he could bring himself to dive again. This time he returned with his and Connie's bags.

He removed her passport and other identification and dumped the bag into the river. He repeated the process with his own gear, then tossing the rifle in. He climbed back to the road and began to run.

He wasn't in the shape he'd been in six years before, but at 30 he was far from being out of condition. Besides, he had learned long ago that it was the mind rather than the body that made a runner; and his mind remembered discipline. He set his pace jogging, concentrated on his breathing. Breathe in four steps, out for two. In, in, in, in, out, out. Four and two, four and two. Keep the rhythm.

He would make the city tonight. "They believed they had killed Nicole Renard, and they would continue to believe it for a time. Henri was the focal point of the hunt now, but for a time even he would be safe," Jerry thought.

They were the only keys to what Louis Renard had called a nest of scorpions. Jerry needed the information, and to get it he must preserve the source. He must track down the Renard's, find them first. He was ahead but the lead was tenuous. He ran, walked, ran and planned. He covered the twenty miles in just over three hours. He bought a bicycle on the edge of town for twice its value and rode directly to the telephone/telegraph office. Five minutes later, CEO of General Systems, a mid-sized Delaware corporation, James Crossman picked up his phone. It was 4:30 p.m. in New York.

This is Jerry, Jim. Where is each of the company's executive aircraft?"

"Why do -"

"Get me the information now, Jim, I haven't time for questions," he ordered, "and turn on your recorder."

"Just a moment, Jerry," Crossman answered.

"I'll check." He was shocked by Jerry's abruptness and the request, especially since this was his first call in over three weeks. Crossman knew where the support for his leadership of the corporation came from though, the majority stockholder. He was, where he was, at one mans whim, and he needn't be reminded. He was back with the information in seconds.

"Jerry, the Lear jets are in San Francisco, and San Juan. Prop jobs in New York and Denver."

"Get on the telephone to San Juan and have that plane on the way to Bobo Dioulasso, Rep. of Upper Volta. It's a Four-thousand-mile flight. That plane is capable of making it in nine hours. I want it here in no more than 10 hours. Have $20,000 credited to me in Dakar, Senegal first thing in the morning, Senegal time. I also want two security types that can be trusted, in Dakar within ten hours. Choose two who are black, and they need to speak some French. Don't tell me that's impossible either. If you can't manage to get them on commercial flights, charter a jet. Also, arrange a contact for me. A man I've dealt with named Hermon de Luce. He's a shipping contractor who often arranges UN shipments there. He's someone who will know the Senegalese officials, the ones I can bribe; police, customs, and airport. I may need information or have problems that need to be smoothed over. Radio the information to the plane. This is no joke, Jim. Don't mention this to anybody, and don't fuck up!" Jerry hung up.

Next, he wrote out a telegram to Connie's parents: *Mom and Dad, have decided to put off visit for a short time due to emergency conditions here. Too much work to leave now. Will write details. Love Connie and Jerry.*

Jerry passed the note to the operator, paid his bill and disappeared into the deserted street. He woke an acquaintance, employed by F.A.O. explaining that his truck had broken down, and he'd been forced to hoof it to town. Could he spend the night?

The man told him to help himself to food and a shower; he pointed out the couch and went back to bed. Jerry laid out the ID's and passports to dry, then showered and had a quick snack. When the man rose the following morning, Jerry was gone leaving only a note thanking him.

*****

Henri Renard's photos had arrived within six hours of Van Riebeek's phone calls. There were no commercial night flights in or out of Upper Volta's airports, so the time elements had not been critical. A police contact had assured one of Van Riebeek's operatives that Renard had made no report of a murder. Nor had any sign of him been seen on the road.

The clerkish man at the airport carefully checked four separate photos of Henri Renard, which were stapled inside his magazine.

He looked away from Jerry Carlton at the customs gate. "Nothing like the man," he thought. It would be a very boring day in a hot airport. He observed the man boarding a small jet and envied the rich. The plane took off moments later. He wished for a cool glass of wine, to sip under a fan. Three hours later he had his wine. Henri Renard had been found and disposed of in the airport lounge at Dakar.

On hearing the news, Van Riebeeck was relieved. Now, only routine paperwork and minor details were required to bring the operation to a close.

3

*Wake, For the bird of time has but little way to flutter
and the bird is in the wing.*
"Rubaiyat," of O. Khayyam

The Lear jet reached Dakar a few minutes after eleven
a.m.   Jerry cleared customs but left the crew with
instructions to fuel and service the aircraft, then stand by
for immediate takeoff. Meals would be sent to the plane.
He met Ben Trapper and Carlos Cabron in the restaurant;
Trapper was black and from Montreal. Cabron was
Portuguese and had spent time in Senegal before. He
explained only that they were to find a French brother and
sister who would have arrived here within the last thirty-six
hours, and that someone else was also searching. The
only lead was that they had arrived by private plane from
Upper Volta. He gave the security men the names of the
Senegalese bureaucrat, and officials Crossman had made
connections with. Cabron would check customs, Trapper
the airport tower and both were ordered not to mention
Carlton's name or General Systems. They would both
receive a $10,000 bonus if all went well and they kept their
lips buttoned. He would go to the bank and police station,
then meet them back at the airport in two hours.

At police headquarters he discovered that Henri Renard had been killed. Apparently stabbed to death when he had resisted a robber. The murder had taken place in a stall of the airport men's room only three hours earlier. There had been no witnesses. His contact, a police inspector sold him what remained of Renard's papers and for twenty-five thousand Franks had promised to notify him of any call by his sister, Nicole.

Jerry returned to the airport disturbed by the speed at which Henri Renard had been located and killed. He'd have to find the girl very quickly. She was safe only so long as they thought her dead, and she was now his only known source of information.

Trapper had gotten a list of sixteen private planes arriving the day before. Cabron found out which of the aircraft the Renard's had arrived on and the addresses of the owner at airport customs. An additional twenty thousand Francs were spent to remove all traces of the Renard's arrival from the records. In Henri's wallet had been a photo with "Love, Nicole" on the bottom. With the photo and the address, the three men rented a large car and drove east into the suburbs.

It was a wealthy neighborhood and the house, like many, was walled. Trapper removed his jacket, tie, and socks, then walked up an alley to the back of the house. The adjoining home was closed and the lawn needed cutting. Trapper acquired a push mower from beside the house and began cutting the lawn. He could see the back door of the adjoining house perfectly. He was in a position to intercept if necessary.

Cabron stayed with the car, while Jerry walked up the drive to the house's front door. Hoping she would be alone, he knocked twice and waited for the door to open.

Her smile was wide and friendly as she opened the door, "Bon Jour, Monsieur."

Jerry grasped her arm, spinning her, pressing the chloroformed cloth to her face. He stepped into the house with her in a vice like grip, and then supported her as she collapsed. He whistled a signal; Trapper ran around the side of the house and together they put her into the car. Jerry placed tape over her mouth, then covered it and her eyes with bandages. Cabron drove back to the airport and onto the field alongside the Lear Jet where the still groggy young woman was manhandled aboard the plane.

When the jet took off five minutes later, customs forms showed: the pilot, copilot, three male passengers, and one female – a Mrs. Connie Carlton. Jerry had what he needed and was determined that nothing would stop him. Research and study, then gather information to know who he would be dealing with. Know them better than they knew themselves. He would enter the sphere of whatever entity had manipulated these actions; he would pull the structure of their organization down on their heads.

"Bete noire! You are one of them; I don't believe you," Nicole said. She sat on a couch at the rear of the plane eyes glued on Jerry.

The panic was gone then; her face was composed. "A beautiful face," he thought. "Perfect cheek bones, lips, fine up curving nose, luxuriant auburn hair tumbling to her shoulders; her complexion was very fair, freckled slightly by the desert. A face not normally cold, but snow and ice now, cool except for luminous green eves. Ice and fire," Jerry told himself. She was strong like the Hmong women he'd known in Laos, proud and dry-eyed before the enemy. Their eyes had been black, but also caught fire when they hated. Tears were shared only with friends.

It took two hours, alone in the rear compartment to convince Nicole. She had been frightened, yet instead of letting fear get the best of her, she took it all in: water stained passports, her father's death, Henri's, his own escape, and the reasoning behind her abduction. It was complex, a difficult story to believe.

It wasn't the facts or arguments that convinced her though. It was a look that came over his face when he described his wife's death, and again when he mentioned the telegram to her parents. An expression of barely controlled anger, horror. Then when he began to describe what he would do with the things she knew, then she began to believe. "He has gone mad with hatred and loss," she thought, "yet perhaps insanity is necessary to accomplish what he intends." She experienced a sort of emotional shift with her acceptance. A relief, a natural protection seemingly denied the man seated next to her and suddenly the cool composure of her face shattered.

Jerry found himself in the company of a totally different woman who had begun to cry softly. He waited for her to stop crying, knowing that she believed in him now, that she shared a sense of vengeance with him; an equal affinity for a hate of the unknown danger that threatened.

He noticed a discolored area at the base of the girl's neck where he had manhandled her and felt a twinge of guilt. Pushing the intercom button, he told Trapper to bring an ice pack and some brandy to the aft cabin.

"Sorry about that," Jerry said after Ben closed the door again. He placed the pack against her neck and poured two glasses of brandy.

When they touched down in San Juan for fuel, Cabron arranged to have meals delivered aboard. They cleared U.S. customs and continued on to Denver where Jerry had radioed for a suite of rooms to be reserved under a false name. The abduction was explained to the plane's crew as the abrupt and forceful termination of a family quarrel. No explanation was given Ben Trapper or Cabron who were experienced enough to keep their collective mouths shut.

After hotel security had been arranged, and Nicole seen to her room, Jerry fell across his own bed fully clothed, and slept. That night, he had the nightmare for the first time.

4

Those who play with fire, Will surely be burnt.

Nicole Renard rose early the next day to put herself in order. One of the hotel shops provided her with a small, but suitable wardrobe, and afterward she had taken the trouble to order lunch for them.

She looked quite transformed, face clean and fresh, hair brushed, wearing a denim suit that accented a striking figure. She was long legged with a high and narrow waist, which flared into moderate rather than superfluous curves. Jerry Carlton was not on an emotional level to take much notice. She began speaking, explaining what they had been investigating during lunch. A tape recorder turned slowly while Jerry took notes.

"It is really such a simple formula. As long as there is upheaval there is the potential for enormous gain over your competition," she said. "The disorder can present itself in many ways. Their secret is to guide and control the chaotic elements. If necessary, create the elements, give them only enough support to stay alive for a limited period of time and guide them, control them by holding back support unless they move in the direction you wish."

"For instance, do you have any idea of the drop of land values in Kenya during the Mau-mau uprisings? The commercial interests that stepped in and bought when prices were at bottom made a fortune. What of industry and mining interest in the Congo during the holocaust that followed independence? What are the advantages of controlling the leader of a small country? What kind of concessions could be gained after putting him in power? Disrupt and control on a vast scale and you create the opportunity for immense profit. People starve, suffer, die, which is of little consequence to those involved."

"My father went to an irrigation project near Wau in the southwest Sudan about three months ago. He was not invited; he was simply poking around for material, collecting data. The project was doing excellent work but was also flying in arms in machinery crates. A cargo plane crashed on landing and scattered rifles and ammunition all over the field. He took several pictures of the crash and departed before the excitement died down enough for someone to notice him and ask questions."

"My father had been around his business for a long time and didn't intend to offend anyone involved in the murky world of the professional arms smuggling. Besides, the real stories are found in the politics behind such clandestine activities, not with the individuals involved in carrying them out."

"My father had been a correspondent in many nasty little wars. He knew when to back away from an incident. It's the little guys, the local thugs who usually have most to lose; they would slit your throat just for insurance. In his world you were only safe once an article was in print but before that, beware. Afterward, we had driven westward into the Central African Empire. French President Valery Giscard d'Estaing had promised to consider economic aid, two years back, for the building of railroads needed to develop natural resources. Father thought a follow up on this might be worthwhile as part of the overall view. We found that no real progress had been made, but that private concerns had been awarded vast tracts for mining and the same corporations were planning private development of a railway system to export the ore. The agreements with President Bokassa seemed so favored that we really became curious."

"An old friend of my father was with the embassy in Bangui and we had dinner. Eventually the conversation was brought to the mining concessions and Cartier said that common rumor had it that officials of the corporation concerned had been instrumental in warning President Bokassa of an attempted assassination a year before. Well, that had explained that, we thought," Nicole said emphasizing the remark with a shrug and continued.

A few days later they had driven West to Ft. Sibut, and then North and over the border into Chad. They were first at Ft. Archambault, and then went to Ft. Lamy. Nicole and Henri had continued gathering famine and relief data but Louis Renard had moved off on tangents continuously. There was a small Liberian backed rebellion going on in the North, and there had been the usual attempted overthrows and assassinations of General Malloum's government. The economy was generally a shamble, but a few foreign companies were investing and were strongly in the favor of General Malloum. It seemed that not only had they been involved in the overthrow of the previous regime but had given Malloum information of an attempt to seize power, but Frolinat only last April. They were now soliciting military aid from France in Chad's behalf. The same corporations had reopened several large mining operations bankrupt during the disorders. The stock had been acquired for a pittance, but the mines were now producing at a large profit.

Two situations so similar had seemed unusual to Louis Renard. He began to research how much of the minerals industry was changing hands, under what conditions, and at what profit. Within three weeks a pattern had begun to develop. At first, he suspected that it was his imagination, then after a few days in Niger he found a common thread.

At Niamey airport, he had been in the bar waiting for a plane that would take him to Bamako, in Mali. He thought a man at the far end of the bar had looked familiar which was impossible, for he had been killed over a year ago in an accident in Alexandria. When he moved closer he was sure the man was Jan Paul Millette for they had served together for two years in Algeria and during the Army Rebellion in 1958.

Millette had been employed as a mercenary during the Congo wars and involved in any number of sordid little military operations during the past 20 years. The last Louis Renard had heard of him, he had been on contract to the Army of the Central African Empire as an instructor. He had fled the country at the time of the Bokassa assassination attempt and his death a week later in Alexandria had been mentioned in the papers. Louis was somewhat surprised to find him alive in Niger a year later, but excited at the possibilities for information.

Millette was very nervous and Renard's unexpected presence did not aid to calm him. As it turned out, Jan Paul was also waiting for a flight, only to Brazil via Dakar. He carried false papers and was on the run, neither of which was unusual for a mercenary. What was unusual was that Millette was terrified.

"Father taped the conversation without Millette knowing it," Nicole said, leaning forward, elbows on the table. "We listened to it, a few days later on his return to Fort Lamy. Afterward he discussed his suspicions with Henri and me. It seemed that Jan Paul had been employed to help arrange the assassination of President Bokassa. He was to identify himself only as the agent of some organization, and to offer support and funds to the group that would take power after Bokassa's death. In this case his son-in-law, an Army Major. In turn the organization was to receive preferential treatment from the new regime.

"Millette pulled his end of the matter off nicely. Gave the timetable and details to his employers and settled down to wait. Completely by accident he found out he was employed by the same people who were already openly seeking ties with the Bokassa government. They had turned the names and details of the assassination over to Bokassa, and only by luck and experience did he manage to get over the border. Not only was he hunted by Bokassa's people, but by his employer's, and the rigged death in Alexandria had seemed prudent, as he put it.

"About three months ago he had gone back to work," she said, "this time in Zaire. The remnants of the Katangan Rebels had reorganized and invaded Shaba Province from

Angola. He had read one of David Bufkin's advertisements for mercenary troops, and had answered, for Zaire, as the Belgian Congo was now called, and a known area to him. Before any mercenary operation got off the ground, several Western nations sent aid, and France and Morocco sent troops. The Katangans fled back into Angola and he was stuck in Zaire without work. In Kolwezi, just as mopping up operations were finishing, he ran into the same man who had recruited him for the Bokassa job. There had been no chance to kill him at the time so Jan Paul had disappeared again," Nicole said.

She paused a moment, finishing the remainder of her coffee. "His plane crashed two hours out of Niamey with no survivors," she said. "Father had begun interviewing various relief agency people about military coups in several countries hoping to pick up more relating information. He felt that there must be a common denominator. He found that economic pressure was brought to bear in a very subtle manner in each instance, but there seemed to be no solid connections. Four days ago, we were in Mali at an airstrip near Bamako. We had the intention of going to the Selinque Dam, and Hydro Electric Project, when he noticed two cargo planes with markings like the one that had crashed with arms in the Sudan. He managed to get some information, and we traced them to a corporation registered in Monaco, where they were leased to an engineering firm in Brussels, Belgium. Attempts to learn anything else were futile. Our room had been burglarized when we returned that night. This frightened us," she said, looking straight into Jerry's eyes. "Missing were all our notes and photos, as well as the tape of Father's conversation with Jan Paul Millette. Father decided it was time to leave Africa. That same evening, we left, driving all night, Northeast to Segou and down to San. The next afternoon we arrived in Dedougou. We used back roads and no roads, crossing the border," she said.

Jerry smiled, thinking that Connie had the same opinion of that area. He winced mentally remembering what had happened only 48 hours before on one of those roads and made himself concentrate on what Nicole was saying again.

"That afternoon Henri and I flew out of Dedougou with an acquaintance of my father's. On the road he had told us we were dealing with imperium in imperio; a corporate Empire with influence within, yet independent of world government. A multi-national corporation, huge in size, or more than one, a group of them perhaps in collusion, cutting up parts of the world, each manipulating its own slice, but all cooperating.

"He pointed out what multi-nationals had done to Allende in Chile. He said that the time had come when corporations were as powerful as countries. He thought to trace these might take years of watching stock and capital manipulations. To figure out what their goal was, to cut through the financial political smoke screens, would be frightening but fascinating. It was work that could be done best elsewhere, he told us. He was to have arrived on the morning flight into Dakar. Henri was at the airport to meet him."

She leaned back in her chair, reflective for a moment; reserved as she had been throughout lunch. "They were my only family, you know, I'm quite alone now," she said.

Jerry thought about his own family for a moment, gone now. "There's advantages to being alone," he said, with certain bitterness. "You can't be reached when you're alone. No one can get to you. You can't be threatened except directly."

"My God! That is madness. Life without alliances? No one can reach you; what you describe is death," she said, disapproval in her voice and eyes.

Suddenly they were studying each other across the table, eyes engaged in a curious sort of conflict. Jerry's eyes broke away first.

"This, for the moment is war, not life, and we're not here to discuss personalities or consider the futility of emotional attachments," he said in a, flat hostile voice. "What you know about the organization or organizations we're dealing with is vague, to say the least," he continued. "The only leads are a few mining operations, and possibly the outfit with the cargo aircraft, but I think that will do for a start. I can follow those leads for a way, but your father was correct. It will take research into one hell of a lot of corporate records to pin anything down. We're going to have to be selective and watch for shifts in profit and control in specific industries. The mining interests you mentioned for a start. What larger groups control them."

Jerry took a deep breath, exhaled with a seeming disgust or impatience. He was less businesslike when he continued. "I knew a gentleman once that thought the world could be hauled right up on its feet, peace and plenty for everyone. I thought that was a laugh at the time. Vargas was his name; his hero was Kennedy and his hope the UN. He figures that industry, technology, and wealth had reached a point where the industrial nations could go in, and the haul third world countries right out of the mire. Even with their ridiculous military budgets, it could be done with relative ease.

Nicole watched Jerry Carlton intently as he spoke, for it seemed a small window into the man cracking open for a moment.

"I was a kid in Boston then. It was a rough neighborhood and I was a rough kid. Vargas was a professor at Suffolk University. He likes to play the horses, and I was a lookout in a parlor owned by a guy name of Carlo Marrinini. I used to listen to Vargas argue economics. He fascinated me. Anyway, he won big on a long shot one day. Twenty-grand. Somebody killed him on the way home for the money and I didn't think much about him for years."

Jerry leaned back, putting his feet up, balancing his chair on two legs. "I managed a year of college in '66, ended up in the Army in '67, and saw what underdeveloped countries looked like. I was with some people that had a lot of influence on me. One in particular, he'd been in the Peace Corps in '65 and '66, he was a lieutenant in my outfit. He reminded me of Vargas. Talked about the same sort of things. By the time I got out of Southeast Asia I was so sick of death and privation that I wanted to do something. Bill had me talked into the UN or Peace Corps after college. I made up my mind to try and improve the world just a little. As it turned out, I ended up financially able to, more than I expected, but that's not the point. In real terms, it seems like nobody accomplishes much of anything that isn't just as rapidly undone. I'm sure I seemed bitter over personal relationships and my work. It's been frustrating. Now at least in terms of my work I can see why nobody is progressing faster than a crawl. We may not be able to affect things much, Nicole, but at least we can find out why and who and look for possibilities. Also, my father's name was Capo. He was Sicilian, and I have to admit to a certain nasty streak in my nature. I was brought up with a rather different set of moral values than most people and some of them are not easy to dispel. So, as you see, I have a double interest in our undertaking. Justice, revenge would be a better term perhaps, and success in my work sometime in the future, if we're lucky enough to find something out. Now," Jerry said, putting his feet back on the floor, becoming less introspective, "How much do you know about economics?"

"Only the basics," she answered.

"Do you know anything about computers?"

"A little, only. My mathematics background is excellent through calculus. Computer theory wouldn't be difficult for me to learn," she offered.

Jerry stood and walked to the window. There was still snow atop some of the peaks. "She would need help," he thought, "but whoever worked with her must be kept in the dark somehow. What he would really need would be several expert accountants."

"I inherited the major interest in a company that designs and operates computers, writes programs," he said, still looking out the window. "We supply world-wide. These days business is storing. Everything is being recorded on computers, so we will search computers storage systems. Pick through files and evaluate what we get. At this point, I'm not even sure if companies I have an interest in aren't involved in this. I – we can't trust anyone, tell anyone. Now I can set you up in a dummy position in our Denver complex. I can have a computer links installed in another location with a teleprocessing terminal connecting it to our central computer system. Also, we hire a few bright young economists straight out of graduate school to collect and evaluate the data. You alone will know what we are looking for, though. I'll act on your information, and feed information back. Only the two of us will have any idea of what's going on. We will come up with some sort of research for cover." He, turned from the window, and staring directly into her eyes said, "Agreed?"

"Agreed," she answered, looking away from him this time.

"First we'll need to arrange a new identity for you. "I'll find an easily protected area to set up multiple phone lines and our terminal then and make security arrangements. Once this begins to move, we won't see much of each other. We'll keep in contact either through prearranged calls, or through the computer system. Never mention my name or your own name. That's important, Nicole, do you understand?"

"You are a deviously cautious person, Mr. Carlton. I will try to be an equally cautious confederate," she said.

"I make all active decisions, you understand?"

"I understand," she said.

"The first will be to get room service to send up some fresh coffee. Once we begin, no restaurants, theaters, and social life. It won't be safe. That's tomorrow, though," he said with a half-smile.

5

"The success of a venture depends very much on the personnel available to the executive and his choices."
F. North, Jr.

During the following week, Jerry began to put together the physical side of the operation. He acquired a home on 1000 acres ranchland in sparsely wooded hills ten miles north of Denver and technicians soon had his computer terminals installed. A trench seven-hundred-yard in length was dug between the basement and an aspen grove on the far side of a low ridge. Six-foot diameter pipe was lain and buried for its full length before being filled and covered. Also, hurricane fencing was erected near the house.

He sent Cabron and Trapper to Miami where a second house had been purchased. They were told to stay put and live quietly. Over forty men, were interviewed, all ex-military, all veterans; he hired twelve who would constitute a security detail for the site. Half were to be on the property at all times; of these two would remain with Nicole. One of the men, a marine MP who had worked with guard dogs. These were to be used inside the fence. He purchased a second computer system in Canada, and had it installed in a rented office under a dummy corporate name. He ripped it out, crated it and had it sent to the warehouse. It was then passed to any empty warehouse and transshipped to Florida for installation in the safe house. There, two telephone company employees were paid enough to retire for hooking up an unregistered terminal hookup.

In a small office in downtown Denver, two young men and a girl were hired on recommendations from the University of Colorado, for work through the computer terminal in that office. They understood they would be part of a study, researching industrial growth trends in emerging African countries. Jerry transferred operating capital to a local bank for Nicole. He then cashed over three million dollars in negotiable bonds through a San Francisco house, and had the funds deposited in a Swiss account. Two days later he flew to Europe in a company jet and removed the majority of the money, placing it in smaller numbered accounts. He opened several accounts in Switzerland, three in Belgium. The following day he flew to Italy and France, opening two small accounts in each country. He left the Lear jet in New York, then commuted to Boston, where he checked into a cheap hotel to get some sleep.

It was dark when he dressed and walked into the streets. The noises and smells of another life swirled around him. He hit a few bars, finally recognizing a couple of faces. He moved up to the counter and bought a beer, combed his hair straight back in the old style, then listened, picking up the rhythm of the place. Jerry watched the man he had recognized take a sucker for twenty bucks at pool and allowed a half smile to creep onto his face. The man turned and looked around at the end of the game surveying the place for another sucker. He was a good shark; it was his living. His eyes fell on a shadow facing him from the bar.

"Hey Buddy! Play for a beer," he called.

"Screw you, George. I want to give my money away; I'll give it to the church."

The voice wasn't quite familiar, and the shark canted the light a little to get a better look. Where'd he known the guy from, he asked himself, dark medium build, wiry.

"Been awhile, Georgi, you forget friends easy," the man said.

Then it came to him. Christ, the kid had changed. "Hey Jerry, ya mean little son of a bitch!" he yelled, stepping forward to embrace him. "Where ya been for the last century?"

"Tour of southeast Asia, since then getting ahead in the world, making my fortune," he said softly as the shark threw an arm over his shoulder. "How's it going around here, Georgi?"

"Ah, business as usual. Neighborhood's gone all to shit though. I'm thinking of moving out to the suburbs," he complained.

"You complain about the lower elements of society," Jerry snickered.

"Well, you know, different crowd," Georgi said, pulling Jerry to a booth.

They sat down; Georgi talked old times a little, Jerry slowly working the conversation around to specific individuals. They had a final drink to better times and Jerry left. He knew where to find Carlo Marrinini and several even less available people now. Carlo had come considerably up in the world, he discovered. Jerry called a restaurant Carlo owned and asked for an appointment. The next morning a secretary called, and told him Mr. Marrinini would meet him for lunch, at the Bay-view Club.

He spent the morning at a local martial art school working out, polishing old skills, then caught a cab to the club before noon. He walked through the entrance of the main building; it was impressive. A large two-story colonial structure, new, with an old look. To one side was a gym and from the sound of water splashing, a pool. The interior of the club was plusher than the outside; varnished wood, thick carpet and expensive upholstery had been used everywhere. A uniformed doorman stood in the foyer.

Approaching him, Jerry spoke in a pleasant tone, "I'm Mr. Capoli, Mr. Marrinini's lunch guest."

The man's expression changed instantly and Jerry was directed to a private dining room overlooking the coast. Carlo was at the bar when he walked in. "Jerry, good to see you. We all thought you got lost someplace. Here, what do you want to drink?" Carlo said, stepping behind the bar.

"Some wine, please," Jerry said, slipping on to one of the stools.

Carlo poured two large glasses while he talked. He was feeling good; besides, he'd always liked this kid; ever since he was a lookout for his old operation on Clary St. He'd been like his old man, Frankie Capoli, who did a job and kept his mouth shut. Carlo had grown up in the same neighborhood with the kid's old man, went to school, and moved into the rackets at the same time. Too bad Frankie had bought it; he was a good one.

"So, tell me, did you get your law degree, or did that money I heard you came into change your mind?" Carlo asked, offering Jerry a glass.

"I got sidetracked, Mr. Marrinini."

"You quit school?"

"No, I ended up getting drafted in '67, put in a few years in the Army. I came into my grandfather's money about the time I was discharged. Went back to college but ended up studying another field. I am involved in business, though," he said with a slight smile.

Carlo was instantly curious, but one didn't ask shop questions in his world. Business was handled on a need-to-know basis. He was sure that Jerry Capoli had not dropped in on him after eleven years just to discuss the old neighborhood, so he waited.

"I have to admit my visit isn't entirely social, Mr. Marrinini. I would like to talk a little business."

The clatter of their meal being wheeled in broke off serious conversation for a few minutes. They moved to a table by the window and sat down.

"You're gonna like this," Carlo said, heaping various foods on Jerry's plate after the waiter had left. Then he added, "Now, let's hear about this business."

"We have a small group at the center of our business that deals in information, as well as making sure that facts concerning our operations do not leave our offices. Industrial secrets. Most large corporations like to know what the competition is up to so they do business with people who steal industrial secrets, blueprints, facts, dates, names or anything that the opposition would like to know. Somebody's gotten through to us. We have an idea but can't be sure yet. A portion of our files were stolen and ironic as it is, we believe its part of our own security and intelligence branch that's responsible. Unfortunately, the names and placements of every one of our industrial operatives, spies – to be more direct, were in them. We can't move on ourselves. Embarrassingly, it becomes necessary to hire unknown but completely dependable outside talent. We had hoped that we might be able to make the necessary contacts through you, Carlo. At a fair price, of course," Jerry added.

They ate and discussed Jerry's requirements. Carlo told him the approximate fees that would be charged by various technicians. They agreed on a lucrative sum for Carlo's time and trouble, and finally shook hands like two good businessmen. After dessert and a few more drinks, Jerry left Carlo Marrinini to make the necessary calls.

He caught a cab to a theatrical supply store where he purchased a heavy false mustache to replace the one he had shaved off. His next stop was a photo studio and a small print shop in Chelsea, where he applied for several passports. They were to represent at least four different countries and would cost a good deal more than the $15.00 fee for a legitimate passport. The forger promised they would also be ready in one week along with a list of other documents.

He spent two more hours working out before going back to his hotel. Around 4:00 a.m. he woke in a cold sweat. He had been under water, tangled in strands of blonde hair as he struggled for the surface. The more he fought, the more entangled he had become, until, turning, he had stared into Connie's ruined face. He did thirty minutes of exercises to relax himself but couldn't seem to get back to sleep. He knew the symptoms of PTS. He'd been there after his tour, so he just laid thinking until it was time to leave his room.

He met Carlo for breakfast at nine.

"Here are your names and phone numbers," Carlo said, passing a brown envelope across the table. "They do not know you nor you them. Next to each phone number, are dates and times that the particular individuals can be reached. Also, their usual fees so you know what they expect. That takes care of my end as per specification, I believe."

Jerry finished his coffee. He pulled a similar envelope from his jacket, passing it to Carlo. "I appreciate this very much, as do my associates, Mr. Marrinini. If there's ever anything we can do for you, just say it, sir."

"I'll keep it in mind, Jerry," Carlo said, thumbing the envelope.

Jerry stood, shook hands with Carlo and, thanking him once more, left the restaurant. He was on a jet to New York City, two hours later, feeling very pleased with himself. At the same time, Carlo Marinoni was putting twenty-five thousand dollars in hundreds in his safety deposit box. "It had been a damned nice two hours work," he thought. "Never know how kids are going to turn out, but Frankie's son's bright. He could use a few smart boys like that himself, and he always had liked that kid."

***

The late afternoon New York meeting with Jerry Carlton lasted a little over six hours, and Crossman was glad to have the details out of the way. Jerry now had an itinerary that would take him through twelve African and six European nations during the next two months. The reason for his trip, would be a supposed look at the possibilities of General Systems' expansion into some of Africa's less developed countries. James Crossman knew of course that the trip was most likely a front for God knows what, but after eight years he felt that even if Carlton's brainstorms were seldom profitable, there was little that anyone could do about them. Carlton's involvement with the United Nations kept him out of Crossman's hair the majority of the time – not that Crossman disliked the man, simply that it was difficult to smoothly operate an organization as large as General Systems and its subsidiaries when once or twice a year some nearly non-profit humanitarian project was dropped in your lap.

Not that Carlton wasn't intelligent, he simply had rather strange ideas on which way the Corporation should go. Crossman had guessed the man to be entirely different when the probate investigators had put together a file on him after old man Carlton's death in 1969. To read it, anyone would have expected to be dealing with a rather narrow criminal sort. Crossman had been among the executives that gave Carlton a rundown on his inheritance and the stock of the privately held corporation and it's assets back in 1969.

Jerry had arrived in Oakland for out-processing sixteen hours after his plane had left Laos. He was met at the Army Center by an estate lawyer and two General Systems executives from the San Francisco office. They offered their condolences, told him of the inheritance, and that reservations had been made for him in the city. For the next two days he listened, as the Carlton estate was explained in financial terms. At first, he had a great deal of trouble in relating to what he had inherited. Events had been rapid and unexpected. Only a few days before, his life had been at the elementary level of eat, sleep, and survival. Humanity, to him, had represented a clan of six men who could depend upon each other to stay alive, and the enemy who had labored to destroy them. Loyalty had been to his companions, rather than his country. His sphere of existence had been the limits of sight, sound and smell; there had been no thoughts or concerns for the future, only the immediate. Objectives were day to day, hour to hour. Past life, goals and plans had diminished to a point of mere fantasy while on opps in the jungle.

Crossman had been amazed at the speed with which the young man had adapted. By the second day, the jungle represented fantasy and Carlton, or Capoli, as his last name was then, sat in control of a multimillion-dollar firm, with his own personal holdings in excess of one hundred ninety million dollars. He listened carefully to the explanations and suggestions. Crossman realized almost too late that Carlton must have imagined the power struggle that had erupted with George Carlton's death, and sensed it swirling around him. From the pedantic statements, gestures, and tones of voices used in advising him of this, inducing him to sign that, Carlton knew they considered him inept, naïve, ingenuous, at the least. They were wrong, though, for Jerry Carlton understood power and pecking order. He'd learned it as a kid on the streets.

Crossman had taken the gamble of his career that week. He had arranged a private meeting with the young man and given him the inside of the company power structure. He'd told Carlton how they would try to manipulate him out of his controlling position and of what it could mean. Crossman gambled that he was sharp enough to understand and want the power that such control brought; that he would be generous and reward loyalty; that he would believe in an honest adviser.

Today Crossman stood at the window, gazing down ten floors, and watched Carlton climbing into a company limousine. Well, it had paid off. The wealth had never been the prominent factor, rather the influence that came with it. Young Carlton had not been about to surrender command of that influence, but neither was he prepared to plunge into a struggle to exert it. At the end of the third day he had told the small group of anxious advisors that he would sign nothing at the moment but would give them his decisions in a few days. That night he was on the phone with Crossman. He had instructed Crossman to have papers drawn up giving himself proxy to vote the Carlton stock. Jerry was to maintain controlling interest by allowing for the purchase of the same percent of any new stock issued, as that which he currently held. Dividends not reinvested were to be deposited in a number of banks payable to J. Noland Carlton. Considering the fact that his parents had never been married, his name would no longer be Capoli; James Crossman was to have all of the necessary papers and identification arranged for, under the name of Carlton. The last thing young Carlton had told Crossman that night was to remember the background that accompanied the name Capoli, in the event he, Crossman, should ever be tempted to undercut him.

The call had been brief and Crossman hung up incredulous of what had taken place. He, a middle level executive, had just been made CEO and Chairman of the Board of General Systems.

***

In the limousine, headed for his hotel, Jerry had Crossman on his mind. The problem of how far to trust him. Crossman was an opportunist; Jerry knew that, but to what extent was he trustworthy. Jerry had to ask himself the question continuously. Need-to-know, he decided again.

The last weeks were much the way he had felt after getting out of the service. His mind then had also been a muddle of thoughts: sad, exultant, guilt-ridden, and lonely. Where from here, he had asked himself. What do you want from life? He hadn't intended to make a career of leisure, yet he didn't have a firm goal then. It was a circumstance he had never found himself in. He suddenly realized he didn't know who he was, the real person. He hadn't been the suspicious, taciturn boy who had belonged to Carlo Marrinini gang anymore, or the college kid. He was no longer part of a Special Forces team, a businessman, a UN do-gooder or a playboy. The gang, college, army, Africa – together they had all shaped him into a personality he no longer understood. He'd wanted to accomplish something good, but for years it had ended up going south. What was left was frustration and anger. Back then, he had one real friend he could always trust, Bill Donnelly.

It was the same now, and it would be Donnelly he could discuss this entire incomprehensible mess with. Some of the rage had left him, and without it there were moments when he was unsure of the what he was attempting. He felt almost inadequate in the face of the unknown and needed someone to assure him that he wasn't indulging in some quixotic quest. Bill Donnelly was presently with FAO in Chad, which was to be the first stop on Jerry's itinerary.

58

6

*"Recon General:
When in unsecured territory always make use of
advance scouts.
A surprise can prove fatal.
From: Dept. of Army Field Manual, FM 25-79*

Jerry awoke and slid the window shade up. They were descending. Coming in low over the sparkling waters of Lake Chad. It was an exciting scene that impressed the eyes with a vision, of a simpler life, a land more innocent. Then he remembered and thrust the realities of the continent back into his mind.

The plane was on the ground five minutes later. Bill Donnelly, a big man, six four and about 230 pounds, was easy to spot. Once through customs, Jerry was whisked into Donnelly's car and driven into Fort Lamy. Jerry had notified him that he'd be arriving through the agency but said nothing else. Bill was his usual loquacious self. He talked about the project, his local girlfriend, and the lousy heat. Jerry waited until he got around to asking about Connie before he said anything concerning the reason for the trip.

After four hours in his hotel room listening to what Jerry suspected and was planning to do, Donnelly was unusually quiet. "You know, we've been looking at this sort of thing on a local level for years and never seeing a thing," he finally said. "It makes sense. Not only that, but I knew a guy, an Italian, killed up north last month. He was a mineral surveyor. He was telling me just a few months ago that a lot of fishy stuff had been going on with the outfit he was working with. They were bought out in the middle of a job that they were on contract to the government for. Afterwards, the only really important deposits were falsified or deleted from the survey reports. They scattered the teams all over hell afterward, but this guy quit and went to work for an independent. Got killed up north of Largeau, by Frolinat Rebels. He was back in the same area, near Mt. Emi Koussi. Makes me wonder if the guy really bought it the way we heard."

"What's the name of the company that bought his outfit?" Jerry asked.

"Hell, if I can remember. Shit! The whole idea of this aggravates the hell out of me, Jerr. There has to be capital investment to pull these countries up, but this type of manipulation wrecks legitimate investment, and keeps the local governments in a constant chaotic state. When you look at it this way, it's so plain it's scary."

"What sort of deposits was the Italian talking about?" Jerry asked with his usual single-minded curiosity.

"Chromium, and one hell of a lot of it, I guess," Donely said, blowing smoke from a now very short cigar. "One hell of a lot of it."

Jerry swirled the ice in his glass, leaned back on the couch, and put his feet up. "Did he work in the section where the deposits were discovered, Bill?"

"No, but he had gotten word on the primaries from a buddy who was with the team. Later the word was that it had fizzled but Vito swore that was bullshit. He got together with an Australian named Lewis, a small independent, and went to look himself. Was quiet about it, but plenty of people knew. If he told me, he told others. Vito had a big mouth, Jerry."

"Look, if we went up there, said nothing to nobody, worked it fast, then we'd know something. Also, I want to check out the name of the engineering and survey company who took over that contract. Be interesting to see who owns them, Bill. Also, you know a geologist you trust?"

Donnelly switched the cigar butt into a waste basket. "Why not ask me for the name of a brain surgeon. Christ! Besides, I'm damn busy. How long do you expect to be up there?"

"Vito told you the general area. We take two jeeps and work hard. One week!"

"There's a war going on up there, Jerry, and you know damn well we're on shaky ground, even with Agency papers."

"We've been in a war before," Jerry said, with the same stubborn single-mindedness that had driven Donnelly crazy when they were in the Army together. "Call it a sightseeing excursion. I've only got a week myself, so how about it?"

Donnelly lit another cigar and chewed it for a minute. "All right, rich boy, a week, but you handle anything we come up with. I haven't got the contacts to mess with this. Anything I can do, I will, but it looks like blind men poking at a hornet's nest presently, Jerr. Besides, I've got all I can handle with FAO at the moment."

"A week should do it, Bill," Jerry said, getting up to pour another drink. If we fly up to Largeau tomorrow, can we get the equipment we need, Bill?"

"Oh, you're a real dandy, Jerr," Donnelly said. "You might find it in a week with luck. Call up one of your pet executives and have them fly out what you need tonight. I know a few of the boys in customs up there. I'll make a call and get your parcel through if you can grease their palms."

"And a rock-hound, Bill."

"O.K., I'll see what I can dig up."

Jerry laughed. That was funny, dig up a rock-hound. "It was getting easier to laugh," he thought. "Nicole Renard might be right. A man shouldn't avoid friends, alliances."

It was an eighteen-hour drive across the east slopes of the Tibesti Mountain Range. They followed a dirt track north through the villages of Yarda, Gouring and Kada; a party of five, Donnelly, Jerry, a French surveyor named De Frons, and two Batha natives. In the late afternoon they turned northwest fifteen miles beyond Gouro, leaving the road and cutting across the north face of Mt. Emi Koussi.

Donnelly talked, as always, about camping with an uncle some years back, college, dance lessons his mother had tortured him with, the Army, and always the times he had had in the Peace Corps. Jerry listened in his usual taciturn manner as the miles clicked on the odometer. They stopped only to gas up the two jeeps, change drivers, or clean out dust masks. Between stints on the wheel, jerry tried to sleep, in spite of the jolting ride.

"Hey, wake up, you grubby bum," Bill yelled, shaking his arm. "Come on, look at the view. It's something to tell your kids about."

Jerry slid up in his sear, squinting into the sunset, and gasped, jerking himself upright. "Jesus," he said, looking over the edge of the seat into three thousand feet of space. "Get away from the edge."

"Don't worry, solid granite."

"All I see on my side is air," Jerry said, watching a boulder begin tumbling down the nearly vertical wall of the gorge, and pressing back from the side.

"Caravan track. Edge of the gorge flattens out in a few miles. We'll get down into it then. Should make it before dark," Donnelly said, hauling on the wheel to avoid a boulder.

Glancing back at the following jeep, Jerry muttered that he'd settle for about twenty feet from there, and Bill laughed.

"Didn't know you were acrophobic," he joked. "How'd you get through climbing in Ranger School?"

"Carefully."

"You're as bad as my old man."

"Come on, Bill, let's not start on your parents again."

"How about yours then, ten years and I haven't heard about yours, Jerr."

"O.K. Sure. My father was born, he made it with my mother, and they died, so here I am," Jerry said.

"A classic and detailed biography."

"I'm hungry," Jerry mumbled.

"I'll stop the jeep and you can kill something."

"Bullshit."

"We'll eat when we camp," Bill said, downshifting and maneuvering into a gully.

"If!"

The scenery for the next few miles held Jerry's attention. The overpowering mass of the sempiternal peaks brought back the old feelings of his own insignificance. Ambitions and values were pulled into perspective, by the granite reality of the mountains. Finally, Donely pulled up next to a rock shelf and checked his map. "Close enough," he said, and shut off the engine.

They woke shivering with the sky turning pink over the pass, but dark yet in the gorge. One of the natives climbed out of his sleeping bag and tried to rekindle the fire. Jerry climbed out of his bag and nudged Donnelly with his boot. The face that stared back from the other bag was slack with sleep, the eyes were bloodshot, and the dark shadow of a beard was pushing it's way through yesterday's accumulation of dirt.

"Morning," it said, cracking an idiot's smile. "Great night's sleep, huh?"

The Frenchman a few feet away sat up, wrapping his bag around him, blaspheming God and his horrid landscapes. They had eaten and begun working down the gorge by the time the sun topped its lip. After a morning of lugging the electronic detector and chipping away at sections of the wall, they were wearing down. The heat was in the nineties even at this altitude, and the break for lunch was appreciated. De Frons assured them that there was chromium in the area, but the deposits were unprofitable so far.

"You can find some bearing rock anywhere around here," he told them. "The trick will be to see if there is a truly rich source somewhere. This is why I believe the original surveys must have included the Gorge, as Monsieur Donnelly had heard. Seasonal floods have been abrading a natural cleft fourteen miles long for a million years. The rock and mineral structure in the area is much the same as the Rhodesian fields. If chromium is in the area in a commercially profitable amount, we should find signs of it here, and for myself, I think the possibilities are excellent."

They worked another eighth of a mile that afternoon with no particular luck. De Frons decided to work up onto a shelf about 75 meters above the floor. Five minutes after he reached the ledge, he clambered down again. The chromium was here, miles of it, and incredibly rich.

They went back for the jeeps and drove down the gorge, stopping periodically for De Frons to take samples. They had driven perhaps five miles when they came upon the camp. Bill stopped the jeep. The other party, caught in the process of breaking camp, seemed totally surprised to see them. Jerry put a pair of glasses to his eyes. The letters on the sides of the trucks were A.S.M.

"That's no military unit, Jerry my boy, but I do believe we had best beat feet," Donnelly said.

"Shit, we should know better," Jerry agreed. "Make it fast, they have a radio. If they are just as innocent as hell, great; if not, we could end up like your friend Vito. Maybe I'm paranoid but too much has happened to me lately."

Donnelly turned the jeep heading back up the gorge at the best speed that the terrain allowed. De Frons had yelled when they wave to him to follow. To run from another group of Europeans seemed ridiculous, and he demanded to know what was going on.

"Later," Donnelly had yelled back, "later."

They had managed four miles when De Frons' jeep broke an axle. Bill turned again and drove back to him. Jerry yelled for the three men to leave it, but to bring the spare fuel cans. Again, De Frons started yelling and Donely told him to get in or walk. They had just begun to move again when Juni clutched his throat and tumbled off the back of the jeep. A split second later the windshield shattered and De Frons pitched forward between the seats with a gaping hole where a bullet had emerged from his back. Donnelly spun the wheel, running the jeep under a ledge where centuries of water had eaten the rock away. The firing stopped, but the echoes took a moment to die away.

"God damn my luck," Jerry swore, jumping out of the jeep.

"What's the manual say about getting out of one like this, little Sergeant?" Donnelly asked, seemingly more annoyed than frightened.

"Run and hide, big Lieutenant," Jerry answered, equally annoyed. He had underestimated the seriousness of somebody's intentions in this area, and there was a good chance he might die because of it. He thought about everything they had done in the last two days and felt utterly stupid. At the very least he should have sent one of the natives up onto the lip of the gorge to scout, as they worked. Stupid, stupid, stupid, he told himself again, latching on to a large canteen and stuffing his pockets with ration cans.

Donnelly was doing the same, and the second of the two natives began helping himself to a few. "I figure we move back down the gorge fast, at least until we can find a place to hole up until dark. Then climb out and run."

"Yeah, if we're luckier than we've been up to this point," Jerry said, grabbing up a pick and starting to move back down the gorge. Donnelly followed, but the native called something to them, pointing up toward the lip of the gorge, and moved in the opposite direction.

"Let him go," Donnelly said, "he got as good a chance as we have and might be safer alone, anyway."

"One thing's for sure, whoever's doing the shooting wasn't in that bunch back down the line. They had to have radioed somebody. Could be Frolinat or their own security, but they sure don't want any information getting out of here concerning chromium."

They had been moving fast for four or five minutes when sounds of another volley of shots came rumbling down the gorge. They stopped and listened carefully for a few minutes, Jerry looking up toward the opposite rim as they waited.

"So much for the Bathas' route," he cursed under his breath. Then turning to Bill, he spoke as he wiped the sweat from his eyes with the tail of his shirt. "This terrain is rough, it's real rough. If we pick a place now and don't move, they won't spot us. Can't have enough people to cover the area well enough. This ledge ends in about two hundred yards and we'll be sitting ducks."

"Thinking along the same lines. Look, there were some small caves back about a hundred yards," Donely said, glancing over his shoulder. "Stay on rock and we'll back track and hole up in a good one. Chances are if somebody does come in we can nail him. If not, we've got four hours till dark, and thirty miles to Gouro."

Donely moved back along the ledge, careful to make no tracks. "Look," Jerry said, following, "I don't think there's more than two hundred people in Gouro. We'll stand out like a sore thumb, and I'm not about to underestimate this bunch anymore. Why not try for Ounianga Kebir?"

"Shit!" Donely answered. "You might make 70 miles of desert on a gallon of water, but I'll be lucky to hoof it into Guoro."

"Well, we'll steal transportation in Gouro then, or on the road. I'm not going to have anyone get a line on us by walking into Gouro," Jerry acceded.

They picked a horizontal shaft about three feet across, and crawled in. Once inside, it sloped upward at an angle of about ten degrees and opened vertically to about seven feet. Waiting for their eyes to adjust to the dark, bill whispered for Jerry to watch out for snakes. Jerry told him to not forget scorpions, and they both remained silent again, except for nervous breathing.

"Say, we must have a natural vent up ahead, or another way out," Jerry whispered after a few more minutes. "See the glow."

Donnelly moved a few yards further in and looked up. It was a fissure opened and eroded by rain. Too small to get through, be figured. They sat down then, silently, and waited. About thirty minutes later they thought they heard movement outside and tensed. Nothing followed though, and they both lay back again to rest and await the amorphous cover of dark.

7

"The will to survive is ultimately an instinct in all of us.
Some, of course, are motivated more strongly than others."
From: U.S. Army Field Manual 25-79

One by one the stars to the southwest disappeared as the massive cumulonimbus clouds rolled northeast out of the Kaouar desert. The Tibesti range rose up to meet them; lightning flashed as they broke against the western slopes; tremendous updrafts resulted, and the damp rising air released it's moisture in the form of rain. Drops splattered on the rock face, then ran together. Trickles joined to form rivulets, which became streams, that ran into creeks, the creeks rushed downhill, until thundering over their banks they became raging rivers, and sweeping everything before them, they roared toward the plains.

Jerry woke up with water spattering his face and realized it was raining through the vent. Dull with sleep and irritation he crawled out from under the vent, and deeper into the cave. Listening to the storm outside, the security of the cave gave him a sensation of safety; the sound of rushing water, a realization of imminent danger.

Bill woke with Jerry shaking him violently.

"Wake up!" he was shouting over the roar of rushing water. "We gotta get out of here. We're going to be drowned if we don't get out of here," Jerry shouted a second time. "The creek's flooding; it's over the entrance already."

Bill was fully awake, but it took a moment for his mind to clear. His hand searched for his cigarette lighter, and he flicked it. The sight of the shaft disappearing into black swirling water caused a prickling sensation at the back of his neck. Even the air vent had become a small waterfall, fed by the storm. Suddenly he realized the water was moving rapidly upward.

We can't get out that way," Bill stated flatly, pointing down the shaft.

"We're going to drown if we don't try."

"Jerry, we'll get smashed to pulp if we swim out into the gorge now; ten to one we'd never make it up the wall. Maybe the water won't come all the way up."

"We have to try," Jerry said fatalistically, looking down as the water reached his feet.   "What   about trying to get up the air vent. I can boost you up; you pull me up to where I can get a grip and climb after you."

"Okay," Bill said and, snapping out the cigarette lighter, he got on to Jerry's shoulders.

Stepping under the vent, Jerry gasped as the cold water poured over him; he felt Bill shift, searching for a grip, then struggle to a standing position, and suddenly, the weight was gone as he hoisted himself up.   Jerry stepped back, pointing his pen light up to where Bill's feet were kicking and scraping for a hold.   Water was up to Jerry's knees now and he began to shake from cold or nervousness or both. Rocks and sand showered down with the water and Bill's feet disappeared. More rocks fell and he came crashing back down the shaft. The water was waist deep now and broke his fall.

"Can't make it," he gasped, struggling to his feet. "Blocked in places; I can't dig and hold on at the same time."

Jerry looked up at the narrow-ragged crack, then at Bill.

"Give me a boost," he said. "I'll try." Hell, no wonder that A.D.M. outfit was pulling out. They had a weather report. He climbed onto Bill's shoulders, repeating the previous maneuver, then squirmed his way into the fissure. Five feet in, it was blocked, and jamming his toes and knees against the sides, he tore at the rocks and gravel with his bare hands. The volume of water pouring in on him made it difficult to breathe, impossible to see. A small boulder came free, landing on his thigh and nearly carrying him down into the cave. He moved upward a few more feet, braced himself clawing at the obstructions again, pulled the barrier of small limbs and rocks clear, advancing upward with a feeling of triumph. The crevice widened allowing him to look upward as a flash of lightning lit the opening forty feet above him.

"We've got it made," he shouted back into the mine. "It's widening up. You'll be able to float up in a minute."

His thighs were beginning to cramp as he dug the last boulder loose, sending it crashing past him, then hand over hand worked his way up the wet slippery rock; like a blind man he felt for hand holds, foot holds, stretching his arms to the limit to find any purchase. A large rock protruded from a ledge, and grasping it he sought to ease himself up. The gravel at its base scattered and, feeling himself launched backward, Jerry thrust out with all the power in his legs, arching his back, slamming his shoulders into the opposite wall of the crevice. For a split second he caught himself, before the big rock struck him in the chest, causing him to slide back another ten feet, jamming at chest level in the smallest neck of the vent.

Jerry struggled for a moment cutting off more of his breath, and then for the first-time fear struck him. His back was against solid rock and the dislodged boulder was jammed between his stomach and the wall in front of him.

"Bill," he screamed, "I'm jammed!" He had trouble regaining his breath after he shouted.

"Jerr, it's up to my neck down here, I can float up to the vent pretty soon. Can I get you loose from below?"

"No," he shouted back, fighting the air again.

"How about from above?"

"Yes," he shouted down, weaker this time.

"I can't stay here," Bill shouted up, a trace of hysteria in his voice. "I'm going to swim out. I'll try to get at you from the top."

Jerry heard him but could hardly shout now. "Good luck," he called weakly, again having to fight for breath, but heard no answer. The rock that had broken loose from the ledge had fallen with him, wedging between his body and the wall. His feet could find no purchase and his own weight was slowly crushing the breath from him. Bright flashes appeared before his eyes; a dark wind swirled through his mind, and he dreamed he was plunging downward again. Darkness washed around him as he struggled for air. He pictured his wife crushed between the roof and hood of the Renard jeep, trapped and drowned the same way. Some of his fear was displaced by a mindless anger, that he was going to drown the same way, and someone was going to get away with it.

Jerry took a deep breath and began to cough. He shook his head, fighting for consciousness, and realized the pressure had eased. Water was no longer running into the crevice from above, but it had risen to his chest from below. His heart raced in panic; he raised his hands to a crack above his head and heaved, but nothing moved. Had Bill made it, he wondered? He shouted with all his strength for the rising water had buoyed him enough to restore his breath. He shouted with terror and insane hope; the water reached his chin. He begged for Bill to save him, but there was no sound other than the lapping water around him and the roar of the gorge.

He cursed Bill Donnelly for failing to save him even as he mourned for him, knowing that he must be dead. Jerry arched his head, coughed and sucked in a breath and the water rose above his nose. All things human and civilized passed from his mind; he reverted to the primeval, the ancient, the animal. He lost all regard of pain, logic, even futility; he became like the beast in the iron trap that chews through it's own leg to escape. An overpowering will to survive possessed him and the only instinct left to man sent a massive amount of adrenaline through his system; he tore at the wedged rock, grasped the crack above his head, pulling with inhuman strength. The material of his shirt tore; his leather belt broke loose; ribs cracked as rocks scraped chunks of flesh from his back and chest. The rock plunged into the shaft below, and as his head broke the surface, his lungs sucked in great gulps of air.

Part II

8

"There is no logic in emotion."
Anonymous

The sun rose brilliant but still cool against the rock face of the mountain; a sharp amber ball of light that could not yet drive the damp cold from the high slopes. A massive tree was rushing headlong through the gorge and the piercing sound of it's cracking limbs was the only sound not muffled by the water's roar. Jerry's tear swollen eyes followed the tree's self-destructive rush as he stood atop the wall of the gorge. His arms were folded tightly across his chest to stave off the spasmodic shivering and racking pain it brought to his ribs. He continued his slow stumbling pace along the rim of the gorge, looking for Donnelly, without expecting to find him. He moved slowly seeking covered ground, in fear of those who had hunted him the day before.

It was midmorning and the raging torrent had become a creek when he found Bill's battered body in a crevasse. He managed to drag him above the high waterline, and after taking his wallet and personal things, covered him with rocks. Hurt and fatigue caused him to rest for a few minutes, and he sat staring at the pile of rocks covering Donnelly. Jerry remembered and began to truly hate. He remembered his first position with FAO on the African West Coast, and the almost missionary-like fervor with which he'd attacked his project in an upcountry section. The faces of people and the pleasure of early successes came flooding back into his mind. Also, the senseless savagery that broke out the same year. He had walked out, he'd told Louis Renard. He hadn't mentioned the screams, the bloated bodies littering the streets. Burning buildings, mobs made up of half-starved youths, grasping the chance to kill anyone luckless enough to be caught in a white skin.

Jerry had started toward the border with a man and his wife. At a burned-out mission school, they had found several dozen mutilated children scattered about a courtyard. The priest had been nailed to the wall to better watch the festivities; the nuns were staked out with the older girls and shot when they had been used to satisfaction. The priest was still alive, barely, and Jerry's companions had insisted they take him with them in the mission's bus. He had known better and told them so. Any vehicle would be subject to and vulnerable to attack. They insisted and he walked. He learned two weeks later that they hadn't gotten five miles. The revolt changed nothing there, with the exception that very few Europeans were in the country now, and the railway that was once planned would run through Togo from Lome instead. Almost all foreign investment was in ruin.

Had that been a manipulation too, or simply a sample of the savagery that lay beneath the skin of the most placid African? He could still see the stone weighted stick smashing against the side of Connie's head, her terrified scream cut off by the dull thunk and the gleam on the face of the black man who swung it.

Only a few months past, Mobutu's troops had been killing Europeans themselves. Killing Europeans, even while fleeing the Rebels in Shaba province. When the government troops had arrived, they had put anyone, even suspected of aiding the rebels, in petrol-soaked huts and burned them alive. In tribal Africa, any conflict was tantamount to mass murder. Anyone who would manufacture violence here was worse than despicable. The havoc wrought by the scramble for political control between the United States and the Soviets was bad enough. But in fact, even they might be drawn and pushed this way and that without knowledge of it. The possibilities were endless and Jerry was confounded by them.

"I'm sorry, Bill," he finally whispered, and pushed himself to his feet.

Turning painfully, he limped downhill toward the flat lands. Even with the falling grade, it took seven hours and almost all his remaining strength to get off the mountain. Even at the lower altitude, the air was becoming chill again. His injuries had made him feverish, and the cold made his teeth chatter. He drank water from rock pools and forced a steady careful pace in the direction of Guoro. Hate kept him going, hate and guilt, for between his own rash stupidity, and the hungry drives of some faceless circle of men, the two people he most loved had died. Twice he had survived. It had been a form of schooling for him, a deadly lesson in the art of ruthlessness. Because of it, he had gained an all-important insight into this malignancy. To combat them he must be viler, more infamous than they. If success in this demanded brutalities and atrocities, he would commit them, for if one man alone must stalk this multi headed giant, he must be inexorable, be ready to use every expedient in order to succeed.

After dark he sighted the fires of a herdsman's camp. Too dizzy to walk, he crawled toward them until finally he was jerked back into reality by the braying of the donkeys, and the strength of the young Taureg whose hands sought to keep him from crawling into the fire. When he woke, he gazed through a soporific haze at an old man with a bowl of stringy beef. He offered it with dignity and authority, speaking at the same time in horrid broken French. He wished to know how the gentleman felt, and if it was permitted to be so bold, how had he come to be injured. Jerry accepted the beef and some water with a phlegmatic nod and told the old man that he would live. He said that a plane he had piloted had crashed in the storm night before last. He thanked the old man for his life, but the old man only smiled.

"La ilaha illa Allah," he said. "It is his will."

Later a woman came and ran her hands along Jerry's sides. He groaned several times and the old man laughed. The woman spoke in a low voice and shook her head. Broken ribs, the old man had told him; painful but not serious, in this case. The family were Taureg tribesmen, proud, nomadic people, and Jerry would be safe with them. Pain and injuries were a part of life and men laughed, made light of such inconveniences.

***

It was two days later when he moved out toward Faya Largeau with the Taureg. They had paused to make use of the rain to better prepare the cattle for sale in the city. The eighty miles overland took two days, and by the end of the third Jerry was out of the country. A week's rest in Nigeria and several visits by a doctor put him in condition, well enough to travel, and he continued his previously planned trip. He talked to Crossman the day after leaving Chad and had him bury any direct information that would tie him to the equipment sent into Chad the week before. The only information would be that the two vehicles were a gift to Mr. Donnelly of the F.A.O. and that General Systems was in the habit of supporting Famine Relief Agencies. A half-truth that he hoped would satisfy at least a cursory investigation.

After three more weeks, during which he was in Niger, Mali, Senegal, Zambia, and Mauritania, he quit. He flew back to the States in disgust. The general trends were the same somehow in every country. That did not present facts, though. Were a lot of competing companies using subversive tactics, or was there really some sort of conspiracy? Could it be purely political? No, it couldn't be politically motivated. It was too chaotic. It was facts, names, and some sort of economic trail he needed; a trail he could follow, and guessing would not produce one. He would return to Denver and work out some sort of efficient system with Nicole Renard. Something more direct, surer, and perhaps out of Africa he could get some sleep without the nightmares. They were beginning to drive him a little crazy.

It took almost two weeks to work out what they would each do, and to make the preparations. The September sunshine filtered through the trees, trickling through the window onto the large table where they sat. The conversation had gone on for the better part of the day, outlining what each of them had accomplished. She was surprised at the contacts Jerry Carlton seemed to have, the conflicting nature of his personality, his knowledge of but disregard for money. The American was a fascinating enigma. Entire sections of Carlton's life were a blank, for although most men speak occasionally of school, childhood friends, parents, good times, he never did. It was as if he had been born an adult.

A child begins trusting everything, everyone until age and experience temper him with a little suspicion, only it was as if Jerry Carlton had never completely trusted anyone. She could understand the mistrust. The loss of her father and brother were an excellent if painful lesson in it, but it was unnatural to her. The events of the last months, particularly last weeks, had affected her more than appearances showed. Nicole was terrified, but didn't know of whom; she hated, but didn't know who. The only person she could trust, that she felt a sense of camaraderie with, did not entirely trust her.

She wished to be consoled, reassured; she wished that he would just hold her for a moment to ease the awful loneliness. Although Nicole vacillated between a desire for vengeance and a fear or wish to simply be left alone, she did not let her indecision cripple her. Carlton though, had a kind of strength unfamiliar to her, alien to a woman because there seemed to be no need in him. He had said it himself. A man who is singular, who has nor professed any needs or attachments, is untouchable. This is a devastating position for a woman to find herself in, so she had begun trying to avoid thinking of him except in relation to what they were attempting. Once she had decided on this course, it seemed to become even more difficult for her. It is difficult for any woman to be separated from all security, thrust into the company of a man whom she must depend upon, and not form some emotional attachment, however tenuous. That he was intelligent and good looking did not lessen the problem.

She continued to make her notes, concentrate on the instructions he was giving her, and put away all conjecture of a personal nature. His last explanations were on how he intended to steal certain computer records, and how Nicole would gain access to them afterward.

She managed to pull him into a bit of small talk about skiing once he had covered the last of his instructions. They talked a little about Vail and Aspen and she told him about ski areas in the Alps. As usual, he was more for listening than speaking. She gave up trying to converse with him and trying to control her temper, went to cook something for dinner. She couldn't understand why she was affected in such opposite ways.

One of the guards had been a Special Forces man like Jerry, and she watched them practice hand to hand fighting methods from the kitchen. Dinner was a somewhat silent affair, followed by a review of the personal codes they would use. Jerry turned in early as usual and left her to herself. "He is an unfeeling, callous pig," she told herself and, clenching her fists, walked to the window.

Nicole watched automobile lights in the valley, then spent a few minutes reading a magazine. Finally, she went to her room, showered and dressed for bed. Two hours later, still unable to sleep, she got up and went to the kitchen to make some coffee. The first muffled cry brought goose bumps to her flesh, with the sounds of struggling from Jerry's room. Snatching one of several pistols placed around the house, she ran to his room. Nicole was not dreaming, it was real. They had been found. She bridled her fear, leveled the pistol, and threw open the door.

In the moonlight she could see him struggling on the bed in an attempt to escape an invisible terror. His face was tear streaked and contorted with horror. In a second, she understood. Not only what she saw, but the man. She wanted to take hold of him, gentle him, as a mother would a terrified child in the night. Asleep, the steel control was gone and he was abandoned to whatever terrors he managed to dispel during the day. Placing the gun on the dresser, she crossed to the bed, leaned over, placing her hands on his shoulders and whispering his name.

The reaction was quick and violent. His knuckles caught her on the left cheek, then in the shoulder with a vicious backhand blow. Nicole collapsed, stunned, across the bed. Jerry was awake at the same instant; however, he was caught for a moment between the nightmare and reality. He pulled the girl up. Her left eye had already begun to puff shut and her nose was bleeding.

"Jesus Christ," he whispered, brushing her hair back, still trembling from the proximity of the nightmare. Cradling the girl's head, he dabbed the blood from the corner of her nose with the sheet. She moved against him as her head cleared, then pulled against him, beginning to sob.

"I'm sorry, Nicole, I didn't . . ."

"Yes, yes, I know," she said, pulling herself more tightly against his shoulder, "I'm frightened too."

Jerry didn't answer. He looked past her, through the window at the rising moon. The mountains looked cold and hostile and he had the thought that everything was pretty much that way. The young woman in his arms had seemed cool, hostile, but wasn't. Maybe it was all in the point of view. He tried to visualize the problem, look at himself and her from without, but it got all mixed up in his head. He could smell a touch of perfume in her hair; the warmth of her body and the racking sobs were too real.

They clung to each other for a long time before the first kiss. It was not a passionate kiss, rather sweet, gentle, lingering. They kissed slowly, searchingly, many times before the sweetness was replaced by passion and his hands began to move across her body. He shifted her gown to one side, cupping her breast, kissing it, thinking for a moment, "How beautiful she is." When he began to pull the nightgown from her shoulders, down over her waist, there was no resistance, nor response. He saw her eyes study him as if she were seeing him for the first time, then with a small sound she came to him without restraint, no snow, all fire.

At the first light of dawn he woke. She was curled against him sleeping soundly. Very slowly he moved from the bed, careful not to wake her. He dressed and left a note explaining that it was time to begin, and he would be in touch within a week. He gave the guard a few instructions, then drove to Denver feeling uneasy. He would have to stop this thing with Nicole from happening. He was determined not to lose again.

When Nicole woke and read his letter a few hours later, he was on his way to New York. She stared at the few cool lines and couldn't decide if she should laugh or cry. There was one thing she was sure of. At twenty-three she had shared love with other men, but the encounters had been mere frivolity. She had always heard that physical love brought people together, but now she realized that to be only half truth. The act was merely the culmination of something which had already begun to happen. Someone had said once that a woman tended to fall in love with strong men who were also small boys. In reflection she found the statement to be quite accurate also. She had found what was for her, the mysterious formula, the ingredients she wanted in a man. His opinions and wishes had nothing further to do with it. She was his. He was a man capable of being ruthless, selfish and cold, but she suspected he could also be generous and kind. Regardless, she had made her decision.

9

"Tiger, tiger burning bright
In the forest of the night,
What immortal head or eye
Would form your dreadful symmetry."
Blake

The store owner grunted from behind the counter. He didn't bother coming to his feet. Why bother, the real money didn't come to his shop because of his sweet smile; it came because he could produce what certain people could not buy elsewhere.

"You have my money?" the old gunsmith asked.

"Yes," he answered, pulling out his wallet. "Three thousand, I believe."

The old man nodded and slid the package to him.

"A thirty-two-magnum automatic, silencer, four clips, one box hollow points, one box explosive shells, and silencers for the other five specified weapons. You're going to have to machine the other barrels to fit those things, though," the old man said.

"I know," Jerry answered, picking up the package and placing a paper-clipped fold of one hundred-dollar bills on the counter. "Nice doing business with you, Mr. Schmitler."

The old man just grunted and counted his money. Business got better every year. 'Crime was a bullish enterprise,' he thought, regretting his years as an honest businessman.

Jerry tossed the package among several boxes in the rear seat of his car, then checked the last line on his list. The first item on the list had been the Lear jet. Over lunch the day before, he told Crossman that he would require the use of a company aircraft for a few months. The plane's crew would not be needed, he had explained, but were to be retained at full salary for the period. His own crew would pick up the plane as of noon today, and as before, he had reminded Crossman this arrangement was to remain strictly private.

***

Doug Raferty and Joseph Grade were both ex-military pilots, Raferty of Korean war vintage, Joe Grade, Vietnam. Jerry had obtained a list of pilots persuasive to clandestine work from one of Carlo's nameless phone numbers and chose these two, due to their wide range of flying experience and desperate need to acquire money. A third and equally important factor was that neither had any sort of police record.

"Afternoon, Mr. Best," Raferty said, offering his hand when Jerry arrived at the airport. "Beautiful aircraft," he added.

"Glad you like it, Doug," Jerry said, reciprocating the handshake. "Look, I've got some last-minute things I want to cover. Where's Grade?"

"He's aboard; wait a minute and I'll get him."

"No, let's go aboard to talk. You're hooked up to airport power, aren't you?"

"Yes, sir."

"Good. That air conditioning is going to feel fine, but give me a hand with a few of these packages first, huh?"

They hauled the assorted bags and boxes into the plane and Jerry opened the bar to mix a drink. Joe Grade came aft from the cockpit and nodded to him.

"Either of you want a drink?" Jerry asked.

"Beer," said Grade.

"Same here, sir," Raferty said.

"Here's what's going to happen, gentlemen," Jerry said, tossing them each a cold can. "As far as anyone is concerned, I'm chartering this plane for a business trip. We are going to be making stops in at least fifteen countries. At times, I will fly on commercial flights and you will make flights to cities or airports nearby. You will be carrying my personal possessions which constitute, among other things, illegal arms, thus my need for this aircraft.

You will take all your meals aboard, sleep aboard. You will fuel up and arrange all paperwork on arrival at each airport. I may, at times, have a passenger. I will at all times use a code phrase at any contact. If I meet you, even in person, and fail to use it, watch out. One other person will have the code phrase, a woman. Any questions so far?" he asked, looking from face to face. Both nodded to the negative.

"The phrase is, 'Things are looking up.' Reply – 'Like Hell they are.' Don't forget them." He took one of the packages from the table and opened it, removing two small packets of documents. "These are complete sets of papers for each of you, including passports. There's also a set of papers for the plane. You will fly to an old Army air Corps base at West Point, Virginia, tonight. Change all the plane's numbers and markings. The Lear jet that we're impersonating belongs to a firm in Texas and has only a one-digit difference in it's serial number, so any close check should pass with the assumption of a typographical error. From Virginia, you will fly to Rabat via the Azores. Your paperwork will show you arriving from Sao Paulo, Brazil. Once in Rabat, you will wait until I contact you. Everything I've said is typed here," he said, passing over yet another piece of paper. "Please destroy it when you no longer need it. Any questions now?" Jerry asked.

"Do you mind if I ask just what we're getting into?" Grade replied. "I mean, I didn't agree to get into anything political."

"Don't worry about that, Joe. This is mainly business. I work for an organization that is being undercut by both physical and financial sabotage. I've been told to find out who, how, and why. Before I involve you in anything beyond what we've previously covered, I'll confer with you both. There has been certain loss of life already, but I was led to believe by the people who recommended you that this wouldn't present any difficulty in your case. Correct?"

"Okay," Grade replied and crushed his beer can.

"And you, Raferty?" Jerry questioned.

"I'm satisfied," the older man replied.

"Thank you, gentlemen. Take care of my equipment and I'll see you in Rabat," Jerry said, and left the plane.

"Christ, he's a cold son of a bitch," Grade said, turning to Raferty.

"I've seen them before, son. Doesn't matter if they work for the government, the syndicate, or industry; they're all in the same bag. If our boy is industrial heat, we have less protection, but less to worry about, so let's get things ready to go. We've got a busy night ahead."

"Yeah," the younger man agreed, "better than flying pot, I guess."

***

Jerry caught a flight to Rabat via Lisbon, as James Best. Checking into a hotel, he changed clothes and looked through the phone directory for the location of Brussels Engineering's offices. There was a city and airport location, but he managed to check each before noon. He drew maps of each, added Polaroid photos and instructions. Both offices were to be stripped of all paperwork, files, contents of safes, etc. the papers then would be used as packing around wood statues, which were to be shipped to New York.

He put the instructions into a manila envelope and carried it to a large hotel near the harbor district. Within ten minutes the envelope was claimed at the hotel desk by one of two experts hired six days before in Baltimore. They would do the job, then use the tickets, passports and visas provided to fly to Fort Lamy, Chad. They would receive similar instructions there and, with their recommendations and a fee of twenty thousand per job, Jerry expected a smooth operation.

Exhausted, he went back to his hotel to try to get some sleep, but his mind was hyperactive. It ran continuously over myriad details, and possibilities. Each time something crossed his mind concerning Nicole, he attempted to think only of the business aspects of their relationship. The harder he concentrated, the more he thought of her, until he finally fell into a restless sleep.

At two a.m. room service called to wake him. He dressed and went to the airport where Raferty and Grade were waiting. The plane was cleared and tore down the runway, lifting. It swung to a heading of south by west to avoid Algerian airspace, then southeast across the Sahara to Chad as finally he slept. The sun climbed rapidly as they sped eastward; rising nearly overhead on arrival.

In Fort Lamy, Jerry repeated his reconnaissance, checking the capital offices of the six largest foreign owned mining operations. He snapped photos and wrote out his instructions again. This would be the last easy one, he knew. In a day, two at most, someone would go on guard. He would go to work personally tomorrow, for he needed someone to answer questions, someone to show him the next step, to give him another target. He had thought about trying Uganda but settled on the site of the DC3 crash near Wau, in the Sudan.

It was a seven-hundred-and-fifty-mile flight and they were in Wau within an hour and a half. He spent the night aboard, after clearing customs, and in the morning rented a Land Rover. He purchased a large canvas tarp and tossed it in the back along with a small amount of food and water, checked his list and decided on the silenced Sten gun, rather than the rifle. In the dark it would be more efficient. He also took a pistol and knife. All were attached to the undercarriage of the vehicle, and he drove west toward the irrigation project taking his time on the almost non-road.

Three miles from the site he stopped to survey his map. He thought the dry wash to the south looked like a good spot, and pulled slowly off the road, grinding down into a dry creek. After a few hundred meters, he found a slight overhang where some long-forgotten rainstorm had eroded the lower bank away. He backed the Land Rover against the bank and pulled out the tarp, spreading it over the vehicle, then staked one side of the tarp at the top of the wash, forming a rude tent, and shoved sand and brush on top. Satisfied, he crawled out of the blazing sun, took a long drink of water, and dozed.

***

Jerry woke to the sound of a truck on the road. He threw an arm across his face to block the dazzling glare of the afternoon sun and sat up. "god, what an oven," he mumbled to himself. Reaching under the Rover, he unwired the bundle of weapons and spread them out. He checked all six clips for the Sten gun, attached one, and pushed the others back into the ammo pouch. He pushed the pistol into a belt holster and attached the knife to his left leg. In his right top pocket, he stuffed a short length of piano wire with a small wooden hand grip on each end. In his left, he put a pair of miniature binoculars, then added a small pouch of three detonator timer devices to his belt. Satisfied, he ate some of his food, and drank as much water as he could.

Waited one more hour, he pulled a poncho-like green and khaki robe on, checked himself for loose or rattling gear, and moved off cross-country toward the project. He walked quickly, aware that the bitter solitude of the savanna was but an illusion. He had known many men whose moments of peaceful carelessness and inattention had brought them eternal solitude and a man alone must be far more attentive. He'd always worked with a team and for a man alone almost any mistake ended in death.

It took him an hour and a half to work his way to the edge of the complex. He lay perfectly still watching the comings and goings for the better part of an hour. Still unsatisfied, he backed off, circled and observed the place from another angle, blinking away the gnats and flies as he brought up the glasses. He was not interested in the storage areas or native barracks. On the highest ground to the east were Quonset type buildings used as quarters by the engineering staff. The Europeans were his targets. The problem would be getting one who knew something, and he reminded himself that these people hand no scruples concerning the death and devastation they were causing. Tit for tat.

Pulled himself under a bush, he waited for dark, mind beginning to wander slightly, wondering how his employees were making out in Fort Lamy. Considering the money, they charged, he speculated they were doing quite well. It would be a race from here out, though. Each party would be attempting to find out who his opponent was in order to neutralize him. Like two armed men fighting in a pitch-black room, each blow would surprise.

The shadows lengthened, then merged into one, and Jerry began to creep in toward the buildings. He stopped every twenty-five meters and listened before starting up again. In the distance he could hear the high yapping of a jackal. Fifty meters from the truck park, he spotted the glow of a cigarette. He slipped the stein gun onto his back and crawled off at an oblique angle to get behind the guard. Here, a twenty-year-old war was supposed to have ended, but old feuds die hard and new ones are easily rekindled in an area that has suffered over a million dead. There must be plenty of groups left with an ax to grind. Some would know that the project was an arms supply point which would mean the place was open to attack. He figured this would mean an active guard and security systems and he had been right.

The piano wire whipped around the man's neck and tightened at the instant Jerry's knee struck him between the shoulder blades. The thin wire sank into the man's flesh, nearly severing his head before he had time to suffocate. Tucking the man's body under a truck, he moved parallel to the building, trying to spot another guard. He found two of them sitting in the cab of a truck. "Lousy discipline," he thought. "Damn, they were set up perfect for shooting." The silenced pistol wouldn't make much noise, he thought, but the muzzle flash might be spotted.

"What the hell," he mumbled under his breath, and stepping up, fired twice into the cab. There were two soft pops, and a solid thunk as one of the men's forehead hit the dash. He froze for a moment, alert for any sound of discovery. There was laughing and friendly shouts coming from the laborers' quarters, the steady purr of a diesel generator near the storage buildings, but nothing else. He began to work his way toward the Quonset huts.

No windows and only one door in each, built that way to make air-conditioning more efficient. It was a bad situation, nothing for it; he would have to walk straight in. There was light filtering through the doors of the first two, and he assumed the dark one was the office, so pulling the stein gun around on it's sling, he gripped it with his right hand, opening the door with his left and stepped in with a quick fluid motion, closing it behind and sliding to one side. Everyone in the room froze, with expressions ranging from blank fear to amused disbelief.

"Hands on your heads, move against the wall," he ordered in French, then English.

They began moving, standing shuffling, backward. Six, Jerry counted. Two of the younger men, very fit, in lithe appearance, seemed to glance from the corner of their eyes to a third for some kind of sign or reassurance. The other three simply backed up in dumb fright. Jerry needed to be sure though.

"When's the next arms shipment due?" he demanded, watching their faces. Jerking the stein gun to one side, he pressed the trigger. There was a coughing noise and the end man's face took on an incredulous look as he slid down the wall, coming to rest beneath a group of three bloody holes. "When's the next arms shipment due?" Jerry repeated, more casually this time.

Looks of pure terror had formed on the faces of two of the men, apprehension, to say the least, on the others. At least three glanced at the smallish gray-haired man standing in the center of the group. "That's my man," Jerry thought, and suddenly they came at him. He squeezed the trigger, hitting some in the face, others in the body as they fell and dived, screaming, groaning. Two had almost reached him but were two steps short at the end of their frantic rush. A half smile came on Jerry's mouth; it was the only part of his face that smiled. The small man stood against the wall with his eyes pressed shut.

"Well, sir," Jerry said, over the click, snapping sound of reloading the machine gun, "it seems as if it's you and me now. I'll ask you one further question, with one last chance to answer. Who else has information about your project beyond the local level?"

The man's eyes were open now; they were cunning, wise. They knew what had just transpired; moreover, that for the moment there was no danger. Jerry could see the man would do him no good for the time being, so he walked forward slowly, suddenly smashing the barrel of the gun down on the man's forehead. He kicked him hard in the solar plexus as he slid to the floor, then bound and gagged him.

In the second building he found two men. One about his own age and size had pulled a gun with amazing speed, and Jerry cut him down instantly. The other man dove for the pistol, but Jerry, rushing forward, delivered a vicious kick to one side of his head. He bound him also and stuffed a sponge in his mouth to keep him quiet, then placed a few pieces of gear and a leather sheath with maps and documents implicating a gorilla group.

'Now, to get these two out of here in one piece,' he thought. He made a quick check outside, then slapped the man to his feet and pushed him through the door. The unconscious form of the small man from the first hut lay next to the building and Jerry heaved him across the other man's shoulders before prodding him toward the purple hills. He was pleased with himself. It had taken only ten minutes. The walk back to the Land Rover took two hours, though. Someone would be onto what happened now, but he doubted if there was anyone left who knew what to do about it.

He staked both men out in the wash, next to the Land Rover, and started a small tape recorder. He jammed a small block of wood into the small man's mouth, between his teeth, tying the ends behind his head so that it became impossible for him to close his mouth or spit the wood out. He took a small battery powered dental drill from its box and began to question the man. Whenever he seemed distant or stubborn in answering a question, Jerry would work slowly, exactingly, on his teeth, exposing nerves, then probing them. Unconsciousness was the only pain killer.

***

Four hours later, he drove out of the ravine, physically drained. His two prisoners were dead and buried and someone up the line would have to worry about where they had disappeared to. The experience had taken more out of him than he'd expected at first but the more he'd learned about them, the less squeamish he had become over the hum of the drill and the muffled shrieks. Finally, cold with rage at what they'd been doing, no longer able to think coherently, he had put a single bullet behind the right ear of each man. When the anger lessened he began to feel sick but fought it off.

He drove cross-country parallel to the road, and a few miles south with his lights out. Several times he had near collisions with rocks, and almost drove into a creek, but he kept off the road until he came to within a few miles of the city. He stopped and waited for dawn when he would not be conspicuously alone on the road, and waiting, he dosed off. Light woke him and turning the key to start the Rover, he noticed his hands, now coated with dirt and coagulated blood, almost to the elbows. He lost the battle with his stomach, leaned over the door and retched. Killing clean was one thing, but that had been disgusting. He had the information he needed, but the memory of how he'd acquired it was loathsome.

He began to analyze his motives again, not that the hatred he felt wasn't enough but he told himself it wasn't the only reason he was in this. Or was his reasoning a way to justify what he had done, would continue doing.

After last night, he knew that at least some of the people here were totally without scruple or humanity. He judged that their employers saw no difference between the planning of an operation that could cause a million deaths, and one with no injury at all, as long as it turned a buck. He had decided on his return from Asia seven years ago that he wanted to help people improve their lives. Well, now he was killing two birds with one stone.

The engine roared to life and the machine headed off toward the road and Wau. He would carry out three more operations, then get out of Africa for a while, rest, and digest the information that been gathered, then plan the next moves to arrange chit, chat with the next men up the ladder.

10

"I begin to smell a rat."
M. De Cervantes

Van Riebeeck was concerned. Each incident had pointed to an obvious culprit, but this was one of the problems. The evidence was too obvious. It had been going on for two months before he had stopped deluding himself, no longer able to accept the premise that the attacks were disconnected. There was a flaw in the way his subordinates had been going about this thing. It was an extraordinary situation for which ordinary means were being employed. He had begun to feel this instinctively in the last few weeks, but to have placed this opinion before the people he was responsible to would have been foolish in the most extreme sense. So, he had decided to begin a broad review of the entire period in the attempt to establish some pattern and had chosen a dozen men of the most resourceful type to carry it through. Adrien Baptiste, a truly cognizant analyst, would direct them and collaborate expressly with him in all possibilities. He briefed the man scrupulously.

"What we have here," Van Riebeeck explained, "is a classic intelligence problem." He paused, lighting his pipe, sending short bursts of smoke into the air around his head. "I run what is possibly the world's finest private security and intelligence operation, but it was never designed to handle the present problem.   We are responsible for protecting certain points, stopping information leaks, arranging the physical carry-through of what is passed to us as mere scenario. We make things happen and look as if they came about for entirely different reasons.   We discover what elements make an individual or group tick, and then act using the knowledge to manipulate. We have always been an offensive organization, therefore geared only to tactical defenses.   The problem, I believe lies in that not only our security force, but the parent organization has come under strategic attack. Subtle in the extreme, I might add. The difficulty is in recognizing and isolating the organization we are dealing with."

"Do I understand you to say that you don't know who is disrupting your client's business?"   Baptiste blurted with unmasked astonishment.

"Yes," the director answered.   Had Baptiste known him better, he would have recognized a minuscule flush of frustrated embarrassment on Karl Van Riebeek's face. "You will keep this to yourself, of course. Your job will be pure detective work. You will go over every aspect of the last months and every possible antagonist. You are to consider all possible motives, and find out whom we are dealing with. I will be the sole recipient of any and all your findings, you will have a staff of eleven men, and unlimited budget and no time to waste, no time at all. Are we understood, Adrien?" the director asked, smiling broadly.

"Yes, Herr Van Riebeek," he answered.   He did not care for the director's smile, for it generally carried far more meaning than mere good humor. "I will begin immediately."

"You will find your staff and a complete file awaiting you, and of course you have full use of our computer system. Good luck, Adrien," Van Riebeek said, turning his back to look out the window. He heard the door click behind him.

An hour later he received a report that their key man in the government of Zaire had been assassinated. All evidence pointed to the nearly defunct Simbaest movement, for Secretary Jumitu had been put through ritual torture. "The same thing again," he thought. "But who? For what profit? Could an outside association, or cartel, be competing? Could some segment of our competitions threatened industries have caught on?

***

The mountains of financial figures bore down on Nicole, driving her nearly to tears at times. Always her leads ended in the same dead ends; trusts, shell companies, banks, never with a traceable individual or groups. The system was huge beyond belief, a monstrous web of corporations, conglomerates, loans, and banks. The longer she worked to put together some pattern, the more she was frustrated. Jerry would return drawn and haggard, to give her a box, a tape, a briefcase, and simply disappear again. The first tape she had listened to had horrified her. It's difficult for a woman, even a sophisticated woman, to experience the agonizing torture and subsequent execution of two men at the hands of her lover. It took her weeks to realize that the experiences were as mentally agonizing for Jerry as they were physically for his victims. After that, he always provided typed transcripts and refused to allow any emotional closeness.

He attended to business, was pleasant, but aloof. He briefed her, listened to any facts she might have come across, and then left. He hadn't spent a night at the ranch since their first encounter. Nicole was hurt, lonely, and angry, all at once, but also patient. She was losing the hatred necessary to fuel this sort of fanaticism and working only out of her attachment to Jerry now. Time and futility were wearing at her, but not him.

Jerry remained focused, obsessed with the hunt; he seemed unable to think of anything else. He applied himself with almost mystic patience, as if he could wait forever if necessary, and was above normal human impatience. He seemed to be weaving an exorable web about an invisible foe, and for every move he made, he left a false trail.

She thought of the Jumitu affair, and wondered how he had managed it, but knew better than to ask. He might tell her and she would regret knowing. Instead, she followed the leads Jumitu had provided shortly before his demise. Nicole had been working with a commercial marketing atlas and trend studies of the copper industry. She spent an hour talking to a consultant specializing in world trends in mineral production, then phoned an economics professor at the University of Colorado. That afternoon, she ran countless computer checks on the copper industry. One of the analysts Jerry had hired in Denver was put to work gathering news related items concerning the World Copper Market. The results were exciting.

The bonus was a similar situation in cobalt, but copper was presently the main factor. Subsidiaries of three multi-national corporations had dumped copper on the market during the past two years creating a glut. Prices were low world-wide, hurting the economies of any number of countries, and the stock of any number of rival corporations. It was done in such a surreptitious manner that only by blind luck had she stumbled on to it.

During the same period, vast amounts of stock had changed hands in the troubled industry as the same firms purchased. Alusuisse Deutsche Metallwerke alone had tripled the extent of its holdings. Now, segments of the copper industry were being disrupted. Nicole had a six-page list, including everything from revolutions centering on the copper mining areas of Zaire and Mauritania, to the August strikes in Peru's mines, that cost the Toquepola mine alone $850,000 a day. How long, at this rate, would it take the copper prices to heat up, and the miners in troubled areas to be forces into bankruptcy? It seemed to be timed beautifully, for as one metal was being forced down, others were being heated into instant profits, and slowly, deliberately, industries were being controlled, each in turn.

Through two transactions in Zaire, one in Zambia, and others in Mauritania and Rhodesia, she attempted to trace the movement of capital. An inordinate amount of funding through shell companies involved in such transactions seemed to pass through several banks. One in particular looked promising. She had no idea where it would lead, but it would be a place to focus attention for the present. It took Nicole the better part of three hours to reach Doug Raferty aboard the plane.

"Tim Gleason speaking," he answered.

"Hi," came the voice at the other end of the line. "I hear things are looking up."

Raferty, shocked at the female voice and the code phrase, almost stuttered. "Like Hell they are," he answered.

"Tell him to get in touch right away," Nicole said, and hung up. If only they could get at the bank's records concerning those transactions. Could funding be traceable to a single source? She wanted this thing over with.

11

"Threaten a man's family and you gain his full attention."
Pawlavich

Wilhelm Braun arrived from Brussels on Swiss Air flight 411 shortly after two p.m. on Friday, and the corridors of the Zurich air terminal were packed with tourists. His main interest was getting to the bank and recording the transactions of the previous two days, for only after this was accomplished could he depart to spend a quiet weekend with his family at Interlaken. He passed quickly through Customs and on to the entrance where his chauffeur was waiting. In his car and moving within a moment, Herr Braun had no reason to notice the tan young man entering another vehicle some thirty meter behind him.

Some fifty minutes later, Braun's male secretary suggested that he might be interested in speaking to a young American banking executive. The man, it seemed, had contacted the bank two days before, but had been referred to the president by Henri Weiner. This could mean a number of things, but most probably meant that the American's business bordered on the edge of legality. These matters were passed to Wilhelm Braun for as the president of the bank, he would be answerable to the Board of Directors for any financial indiscretions. This did not by any means suggest that he would turn down a profitable piece of business over mere legality, rather that it was his responsibility to arrange all transactions in such a way as to obviate the possibility of any illegality coming to surface.

Wilhelm Braun nodded and the young man was shown in.

"Mr. Truduo," Braun said, pleasantly. "I'm very sorry if my absence has inconvenienced you.

"Not at all, sir," Jerry answered. "I've been enjoying my stay in Zurich immensely, but – now may we get down to business, sir?"

"Of course," Braun said, thinking the young man a bit direct. It was only polite to socialize for a moment.

"I have been asked to query you on the opening of a series of numbered accounts. The sum involved would be in the area of sixty million to begin. The money will be transferred in the form of bearer certificates. My clients have specified investments in mind but want them handled here."

"This can be arranged, of course, Mr. Truduo," Braun said, "thinking it strange for one so young to be trusted with arrangements for such large sums." "Can you inform me at this time what sort of use these funds are to be put to?"

"I apologize, sir, but I am not privy to that information. The capital has been put together by a somewhat irregular group, and from what I'm led to believe, the money does not exist, if you catch my meaning. I was instructed to contact a representative of this institution and make arrangements for the accounts. I am to gain assurance that a single individual within the institution will have access to the names belonging to the numbered accounts."

"You can be assured of the secrecy of this institution, Mr. Truduo," Braun said in his most dignified tone.

"Yes, sir, but my instructions were to be assured of the secrecy and discretion of one man within the institution. The specific person who would handle all the transactions. It was alluded to me that you that you might willingly attend to these accounts personally. The amount could run near the billion-dollar mark eventually, sir. Some of the transactions might be termed extraordinary, and your name was discreetly mentioned by a party with a similar arrangement. I repeat, they were most discreet," Jerry said, noticing a slight paling of the banker's complexion.

"You have credentials," Braun said abruptly, his tone much less cordial.

"Yes, of course," Jerry said, opening his briefcase. He was absolutely sure now. Wilhelm Braun was one of their bankers. The careful research of the last two weeks, the surveillance of the bank's top officers was paying off. He had been confident before trailing Braun to Brussels, confident enough to have his family kidnapped, secured, and photographed this morning, but not positive. He passed the envelope to Braun.

"My God!" the banker exclaimed in horror, as he removed the family portrait from the envelope.

"Before you are tempted to consider rash decisions, Herr Braun, look at a few of the other pictures," Jerry said calmly, as any salesman might, while making a pitch with a new line of stock. The banker gasped, turning an unhealthy gray, at the sight of the charred bodies of European settlers in Rhodesia and massacred blacks in Mawali.

"If I were you, I should concern myself only with the fact that your loved ones are alive and safe, even if somewhat uncomfortable, for now."

"You are mad! Mad! How dare you!" the banker sputtered, beginning to rise from his seat.

"Yes, I believe you're right," Jerry said, leaning back in his chair. "You see, one of those pictures is a portrait of my family," Jerry lied. "I have very little left to me now, Herr

Braun; a man of your perspicacity should grasp my meaning. My intent is not to vituperate you personally, sir, but I am a vindictive man. It seems that the miscreants responsible for what you see depicted in those photos are numbered among your colleagues."

"What has this to do with my family?" Braun asked in a hoarse whisper.

"Nothing, so long as you furnish me with information dealing with certain numbered accounts."

"I will n-n-not do any s-s-such thing," Braun stammered.

"Then your family will perish in four hours, sir," Jerry said, half-smiling, "and you will precede them by three hours and fifty-nine minutes." He pulled a thirty-two-caliber pistol with a silencer from his coat, pointing it directly at Braun's nose.

Braun went completely gray and large beads of sweat appeared on his forehead. He had divined the man as unstable, as a dangerous psychopath, and it was confirmed.

"What exactly do you wish to know?" Braun asked.

"The names or businesses connected with four numbered accounts, sir. In both directions, paying and receiving, and any other accounts in the same sphere. I want to know the entire scope of your information dealing with your contacts in Brussels and all computer codes for your bank. I also want Three hundred thousand or a corresponding amount in dollars, all old money," Jerry said.

"I will get you the money and the information," Braun said, now completely cowed.

"Oh, I might add, Herr Braun, your family is no longer even in Switzerland. If there is any problem whatsoever – Jerry paused, then gestured grotesquely.

Braun nodded, and pressed the intercom on his desk. When his secretary answered, he gave him instructions for the withdrawal of bank funds, part for the transaction with Mr. Truduo. He himself would handle the paperwork.

"We will go to the vault files," Braun said.

"Thank you, Herr Braun," Jerry answered, standing. "You cannot imagine how I have looked forward to this."

The files were in a safe within the huge bank vault. Only Braun and the Accounts Director had the combination. Only Braun had the keys to certain special files. Almost thirty minutes were needed to check portions of the files. Jerry removed all of the microfilm copies to his briefcase. When they returned to Braun's office, a minor bank official and a guard were waiting with the money. Braun signed a receipt and dismissed the two men.

 Call for your car now, sir, and have your secretary make reservations for dinner for two. The Zurich House in thirty minutes," Jerry ordered.

Thirty minutes later he entered the front, and left by the rear of the Zurich House, climbing into an unoccupied van. Ten miles outside of Zurich in an empty meadow, Jerry began to ask Wilhelm Braun more pointed questions. At first, he asked questions he already knew the answers to and punished Braun severely for each incorrect reply. Then he began to slip in questions that he needed real answers to. He had obtained the names of two more men and was trying for a third when Braun's heart failed.

Jerry leaned back against the engine cover for a moment looking at Braun's body. The corpse's dead eyes were staring back. "How many had that been?" he wondered. He pulled the plastic makeup from his face and removed his wig. Ten minutes later he dumped Braun's body into a crevice, then drove to the airport. He put the briefcase full of money in a locker, the key in an envelope and went to a phone. He dialed a number and waited.

"Ja," answered a man's voice in German.

"Let the Braun's go; we have the cash. It is in a locker at the Zurich airport. The key is taped under the counter of phone booth 14-B6. If any member of the family is harmed, your names will be published. Do you understand?" Jerry asked.

"Jawohl," the voice replied.

"Then get to it and make sure you say only what you were told".

He hung up and took off his gloves as he walked through the terminal. Outside he continued down to one of the private hangers, thinking to himself, "Let them try to figure this one out." The only possible lead would be to the three kidnappers who had never seen him and didn't know him. It would be in all the papers tomorrow as a murder-kidnapping and should offer interesting if incorrect reading for a few days, anyway. In the meantime, he was very near the last steps, to the top. Soon he would have real faces and the reasons and motives that were in the minds behind those faces.

12

Have you not seen the partridge quake?
Viewing the hawk approaching nigh
She cuddles close beneath the brake
Afraid to sit, afraid to fly.
                        -                    ***Prior***

All the latest reports from Rhodesia were spread across his desk; the remnants of breakfast sat on a tray to one side. Van Riebeeck finished putting his own verbal summary and opinion on to tape. He placed the cassette into an envelope, sealed it, and hit the buzzer calling his secretary. She removed the breakfast tray as well as the envelope.

He had been at work since four a.m. as was his usual practice, in order to have his intelligence data read, construed, and sent off to the proper parties in the form of a brief report and opinion. This would allow the executives of various companies an edge over their competition. It was always helpful to know ahead of time, the when and where of political upheaval or economic disasters. Making them happen helped. He opened a last folder, with ADROIT printed boldly across the face. He wondered what Adrien had come up with in the last day. The first twelve days had been singularly unproductive in Van Riebeek's opinion, but analyst like Baptiste would generally show little success until some key piece fell in place. Then all the other sections of the puzzle would already be in place.

November 14, 1977
From: Chief Special Security Group
To: Director
Subject: Code-Adroit

Continued research has turned up no evidence of rival commercial interest as yet. We have covered this aspect of the problem in depth and believe it is not worth following further, except in the most cursory manner, at this time.

We have drawn from sources in eighteen national intelligence organizations including Russian KGB, American CIA, French SDECE, British SIS, Israeli ISO, Egyptian CSP. None have any record or rumor of a national or political movement of this sort.

We have checked contacts with almost thirty terrorists' groups. We did confirm two incidents. One, the ship blown up at Luanuna, was the work of a Maoist group. Two, the mine blown up and flooded in Rhodesia was the work of one of our own groups in Malawi. Both cases were disjointed incidents: the latter was a mistake.

We have had one rather exciting development. On checks of all custom records of aircraft and passengers entering and leaving areas in question before or after incidents, we discovered a possibility: A private jet aircraft belonging to the Texidron Corporation of Houston, Texas. Records show that plane at or near twelve of the eighteen points within the forty-eight-hour period surrounding each action. We suggest you check out this aircraft and it's owners.

A list of passengers and crew are:
Pilot – Tim Gleason – American
Co-Pilot – Jeff Wright – American
Pass. – Jonathan Best – American
Pass. – Alex Pringle – American
Pass. – David Rothschild – Israeli
Pass. – Rudiger Hoffener – German
Pass. – Marco Rodalfo – Italian

We also have a record of a Joseph Niglio and William Jessup, American tourists arriving and departing, six locations where there were either fires or robberies at corporate offices.

I await further information on these individuals.
Yours respectfully,
Adrien Baptiste

"Ho, ho!" Van Riebeeck laughed. "I have something solid now," he thought, "a place to grasp this shadow." He pressed the intercom button and snapped a series of orders to his secretary. Thirty seconds later, as an afterthought, he told her to have coffee sent in.

Within minutes, three of his section chiefs were on a phone line with him, and he advised them that a list of names and instructions would be coming in on their computer terminals. They were to check the men and all aspects of their background immediately. Get everything they could on Texidron, and also query Texidron, as a ruse, on the possibility of chartering the Lear jet owned by their company, etc.

"I want the rundown by tomorrow morning four a.m. Brussels time," he stipulated. "Go to work, gentlemen."

Opening his desk, he removed a can of tobacco, and filled his pipe. His coffee had arrived with the morning newspapers and he took a sip, grunting constantly. "Another difficulty was about to work itself out," he thought. He lit the pipe and picked up the first paper. Bold headlines leaped out at him; William Braun smiled smugly from below the lines "

MURDER, KIDNAPPING, PRESIDENT OF ZURICH BANK, DEAD."

The pipe fell from his mouth, and he stood, knocking his chair backward. This was too much. He strode from the office clutching the newspaper; and ran down two flights of stairs bursting into Adrien Batiste's office.

"Herr Van Riebeeck," Baptiste said, standing, somewhat startled by the abrupt entry.

"Read this and check the Zurich airport to see if that damned plane has been there in the past few days. Unless I am mistaken, we have run out of time," the big man said.

***

The co-pilot sat in the rear of the plane reading a Playboy magazine. Several other Playboys, and a few

Oui's, lay scattered near. Doug Raferty lay back staring at the material overhead.

"Jesus fucken Christ," Grade yelled suddenly, "I can't stand this anymore. I haven't been more than a hundred yards from this plane in two and a half months."

"Take a cold shower."

"Cold shower, hell, Doug. I never had to put up with a screwy set-up like this in my life. I had fifty times more freedom when I was a military pilot."

"Yeah! Didn't we all, Joey." The older man said, conjuring up thoughts of a misspent youth.

"That's not what I mean. I'm quitting when Best gets back. I'll stay until he gets a replacement, then I quit."

"You're going to quit five hundred bucks a day. You nuts, kid?"

"Yeah, I guess so, but I haven't liked this set-up from the start. We don't even know what we're doing yet."

"You're wrong, Joey. We're flying the man's plane for fifteen grand a month, which is the best and safest money we've ever made. That's damned near two hundred thousand a year, apiece; Joey, that's tax free; that's coin."

"Screw it, I'd like the time to spend a little of it."

"Well, hold your horses, we're due to fly to the States in a few days. Ask for a day off."

"Yeah, maybe," Grade said. "Man, I can't get that big broad in Switzerland off my mind. Christ was she built, and I couldn't even try. God!"

"Well, look out the window. There might be a few goodies around here," Raferty said, thumbing at the port, and chuckling to himself. He could remember when he was young and horny. That had been a few years back, though.

"I don't give a shit," Joe said, standing up. "I'm going out for the night. If he doesn't like it, there's plenty of other employment to be had."

"You're a grown-up, Joey."

"Yup," Grade said, and putting on his jacket, left the plane. Amsterdam was a damned fine town to spend a night in.

He was as far as the gate when he realized he'd forgotten his wallet. Mumbling under his breath, Grade started back toward the plane.

There was a car alongside one of the service buildings about two hundred yards from the Lear Jet. Two men were moving from the direction of the car, but not in a straight line. They had made a wide arch to approach from directly aft. Panic seized him for a moment. Somebody was after him and he had no idea what for. If they were of the same caliber as Best, he was in trouble. Grade's first thought was to get the hell out; however, he remembered that not only was his wallet and false I.D. aboard the aircraft, so were his real papers.

That settled it. He ran along the fence for a hundred yards, then into the hangar, emerging on his hands and knees thirty feet behind the car. It took him a few moments to control the trembling that had begun the moment he had stopped at the rear of the car. He removed his shoes and crawled alongside the door on the driver's side. Grade took a deep breath, wondered how he got himself into things like this, and leaped up, ramming his right arm into the car's interior. The automobile's sole occupant was armed, but never had a chance to reach for his gun. Grade, ferocious with terror, had pulled his head through the window by the hair, and punched him several times without knowing the first blow had knocked him out cold.

Opening the door, Grade removed the man's gun, a big Browning forty-five automatic. He shoved the limp body on to the floor, then, climbing in, he started the car, allowing it to ease forward. The two men he had observed were under the aircraft, unscrewing the cover for the air vents. He could see one of them had a small cylinder. 'Gas or a bomb,' he thought, 'and I could be in there.' He considered the problem for a moment, then chuckled to himself. The last thing they would want was attention. He opened the door, crouching aiming the big pistol between the body and the door, then switched on the headlights.

The first thing the man under the plane did was blink and drop his screwdriver. 'What is that fool driver doing,' he wondered. There was a shot, a buzzing sound near his ear, and he knew he was in trouble. His partner dropped the cylinder and ran, keeping the landing gear between him and the car. The man who had lost his screwdriver, tried to run too, but tripped over the cylinder. Another shot screeched off the cement a foot from his head. The logical part of his mind told him to return fire and cover himself, but he had been surprised, unnerved, and made to feel like an insect exposed to the light of day. He ran for his life, overtaking his accomplice with ease as the banging continued behind him. When the jet took off five minutes later, and without clearance, he knew he was in even more trouble.

Doug Raferty was as frightened as Grade had been. He almost hadn't let the co-pilot aboard and had taken off on a taxi way, buzzed half the city, nearly colliding with a radio tower. He was halfway to New York, flying at under three hundred feet above the water, before he remembered the envelope that Best had left in case of something unexpected.

He had the code number memorized and Grade was flying so he went aft, pulled a panel off the bar, and removed the envelope from behind an electrical diagram. After a few moments of work, he had a latitude and longitude, the phrase, 'Wait at phone booth #425-6729 at eleven a.m.' and a local chart. He told Grade to change course and four hours later they were on the ground at an abandoned airfield in North Carolina. It would be eleven hours before the time stated for the phone call, and Grade sat and fidgeted. For the moment, Raferty felt safe. The flight had soothed his nerves for it was much like returning from a sortie when he was a military pilot. He flopped down on the couch and began to study the material on the overhead. The money was good, but his luck would run out if he kept pressing it, he decided. He would grab one last big one and quit. He was tired.

It had been a few minutes past eleven when Raferty answered her call. The man answering had startled her in the midst of what had become an automatic and boring daily chore. Suppressing the onset of fright, she reeled off the code phrase.

"Things are looking up."

"Like Hell they are," Raferty replied, and then added, "And that's a fact, Ma'am."

He had explained what had happened, and she had given him the instructions Jerry had written out in case of the plane being discovered. The aircraft was to be stripped of all the gear Jerry had stored aboard and the arms were to be shipped to a warehouse in Florida. They were to call a company in Raleigh who had been hired to strip and repaint the plane. It was then to be flown to New York, and a small private airport on the Hudson. The airport was uncontrolled and had a small hangar. The jet was to be locked in the hangar and bags of dust stored in a shed outside were to be dumped into the hangar vents over a period of an hour. Once the dust had settled, no one was to enter the hangar. They were to drive to Boston, then take a commercial flight to Miami under their own names and register at the Conrad Hilton. They would receive expensè money and full salary during their stay at the Hilton. Someone would be in touch.

***

Nicole hung up the phone without waiting for a reply or questions. She departed the phone booth as if it had been full of hobgoblins.

There was the unlikely possibility that the voice had not belonged to Jerry's pilot. Anyone who could get that far, could have a call traced to this phone booth. This is why Jerry had set things up so she would do the calling from random phone booths, rather than the ranch. Nicole's speculation on what might have happened got her nowhere. She was plagued by the combination of worry and lack of information. Halfway back to the ranch, she ordered the guard to pull up at the next phone booth. She had forgotten to place her other calls.

He pulled into the parking area a convenience store and she went to a booth. On the third call, an overseas call, the phone was answered on the first ring. She gave the code phrase and there was a click. A voice said, "This is the operator, hold the line while I replace your call, please."

She hung up immediately. My God, what's happening? The reply had been in Dutch, but that had not been an operator. She was sure. She put through the last call and jumped inwardly when it, too, was answered.

"Things are looking up," she said.

"Like hell they are," a voice replied.

"Things have gotten a bit sticky in Holland, and I think it's time that I went elsewhere to make a buck, Honey. Would you please have Mr. Best put the cash in my usual account?"

"What happened?" Nicole asked, feeling foolish. She didn't even know whom she was talking to.

"Whatever tune you people have been dancing to, the jig's up. They were laying for us this time, and they ain't just messing around. I can't be sure, but I think they nailed the second story man that was going to get me in. Give the man my regards, cause I'm going on a long vacation," he said.

There was a click and Nicole stood frozen, with the phone in her hand. Should she stay or get out, she wondered. If only Jerry would get in contact. What if they had him? It was quite possible, she admitted to herself, and decided to give him twelve hours before she disappeared.

13

"And there was light."
Old Testament

At seven-thirty P.M. on September thirteenth, Franz De Hartog was a split-second from death, but quite unaware of the fact. He pulled out to pass a slow truck on an upgrade, inadvertently saving himself. The man now staring at the blank side of a truck through the cross hairs of a rifle mounted four power telescopic sight, swore to himself. He rolled from the prone combat position and retreated into the brush.

"Of all the dumb luck," Jerry mumbled, then shouted as loud as he could, "screw you, you lucky bastard." He broke the rifle down, stuffed the pieces into his pack, walked thirty feet to a motorcycle, and started it.

Five minutes later, he roared up behind the Rolls, but it was too late. It turned and passed between the portals of a big gate and two austere guards. "Three times today I've fucked up," he thought. "Those gold-plated safe crackers of mine will be into Trans-Netherlands's offices tonight, and I'll be out of luck." He knew it could be a couple of months before he would get another chance at the old bastard once they hit that office. He was one of them, that old man, was a regular prince of greed, and the only key man that Braun had known.

Jerry pulled the big BSA off the road and climbed a tree for a good look at the estate. Sometimes, when he thought about them, he wanted to rip them, tear them, stab and torture them, while at others he thought that would be too quick. On another level he knew he wasn't quite sane, for what sane man could even attempt this, he reflected, as he studied the place from the top of the tree. 'I'm thinking like a sadist. This isn't for pleasure, this is to eradicate a disease; it's got to be quick, simple, and without emotion.' He wondered if he was feeding himself a line. 'Rationalization is an illness,' he told himself.

When they turned the dogs loose, he mumbled, Shit." The word echoed through the trees and made a mental note to get a grip on himself. He'd better keep his mouth shut. Also, he was slipping back into the use of rotten language he'd spent years exorcising from his vocabulary. He climbed out of the tree and advanced to the wall. Then walked parallel to it until he found an overhanging limb. He cut several small limbs from a tree, binding them to his left forearm like a splint, then slipped an eight-inch commando knife into his belt. He would pick off all the dogs, if possible; however, if one or two of the animals remained with him on the wrong side of the wall, he wanted to offer them something un-painful to chew on while he knifed them. He appreciated this little trick and several others Sergeant Bailey had taught him. Education is invaluable, he told himself, and began to climb the tree.

Franz exited the room in a storm of concealed frustration. The old man would not take any of his advice and he was going to get himself killed. Franz was sick of the superior gaze and curt dismissals. He was Dutch and considered the old German's military attitude so much garbage. His employer believed himself above danger, but Franz knew Grousmien's dauntless demeanor was based on the false premise that he was too important to kill. Franz supposed a lot of powerful, but mortal, men had shared the same premise, before the ax had fallen.

They had not been De Hartog's responsibility, though. His job was not merely to drive Herr Dr. Grousmien from place to place, but to keep him free from harm and irritation. Unfortunately, all efforts toward security irritated Herr Grousmien, which caused Franz to find himself in a periodic conflict of interest. Today had been and continued to be one of these difficult periods. He could not even get the man to stay clear of the windows.

Franz went to the kitchen, poured himself a glass of wine, and cut a large slice of cheese. He sighed and longed for the quiet order he had known as a policeman in

Kesselborg. The wages had been disgusting, of course, but then, eh! He pushed the intercom button near the door and said, "Report." There were six bored replies. "Danke," he said and strolled to the cupboard to cut a slice of pumpernickel.

The information that some maniac might be trying to kill Dr. Grousmien could be correct, but as long as he stayed within the house, he was quite secure. Franz would not think of going outside with the dogs loose. Anyone attempting to cross between the fence and house would be ripped to pieces. Even if a man managed to kill the perimeter dogs, two others were trained to remain within a few feet of the house. The only way would be to shoot Grousmien from behind the wall. The windows of the private rooms were bullet proof which was good but not certain. On his way to his quarters, he speculated the possibilities of getting Herr Grousmien to pull his drapes, and judged the odds impossible, so forgot about it. He washed and settled into bed, to read his newspaper. The paper was full of American political news. Childish, he thought, and moved to a petroleum article.

***

Jerry lay still for ten minutes after he shot the fourth dog. The 25-06 Ruger-Carbine made up in velocity for what it lacked in caliber and the dogs had all died instantly. He lowered himself from the limb, dropping the last five feet to the ground. He would take the gate from the inside; the guards wouldn't be watching the inside. He was already moving toward the gate when he changed his mind. Those men would be linked to a central location and a missing link would cause instant problems. Besides, Grousmien used a local security agency and these men most likely had nothing to do with their employer's business. He decided to take a chance and leave them alone.

The second dog almost got him. He saw the first big Doberman standing like an evil statue near the house, and dropping to one knee, shot it just behind the right shoulder. It fell, kicking, without a whimper, and he fired a second time, killing it. He was experiencing a mixed feeling of respect and relief at the dog's trained silence, when he caught a flickering glimpse of his own death to the left. More from reflex than logic, he threw his left arm up to protect himself.

A guard dog is trained to go for the throat but grabs the arm if it's thrust forward. The dog's teeth clamped down on Jerry's stick lashed forearm, and its momentum carried him over backwards. He pulled his knife, but the dog was gripping his arm, dragging him backward off balance, and he couldn't use the weapon. Finally, digging one foot into the grass, he jerked the dog toward him, slashing, but the Doberman released the arm. It backed off, ran to one side, striking like a black, four-legged cobra, but this time he was ready. He threw up his left arm and as the dog clamped down, he drove up under it with the knife. He stabbed twice more after the animal let go, then dragged it into the shrubs where he sat trying to catch his breath.

"Jesus," he whispered, panting. "Luck's getting thin." A few minutes later, he was on the roof. He pried a screen loose and removed an exhaust fan to open an entrance into the attic. There had been pigeons inside and the rapid fluttering had given him another bad scare. He wondered if his nerves were starting to go.

He found the attic door and moved down into the house. He wished he had had enough time to have contrived a solid subordinate plan. He had intended to shoot the tire on Grousmien's car and then the driver, when the car stopped; that way he would have had the man by himself with little chance of personal danger. A direct attack on the man as he was driven down a highway was safe if not exactly subtle; however, he knew going after him at home among staff and guards was just stupid. He had survived so far due to surreptitious plans and the use of every subterfuge in carrying them out but time had run out.

He had left the rifle outside and now carried only the pistol. Grousmien probably kept a night staff, so he'd better find them first. A television set was on in one of the downstairs rooms. It was always possible that someone on the other side of the door had a gun. He hated going against a series of unknowns like this. Pushing it quickly open, he stepped through.

The startled maid dropped her coffee, and her companion, an older man, let his mouth hang open at the sight of the gun. Jerry motioned them into the corner, had them lie down, and tied and gagged them with curtain cord. He hadn't noticed the old man push the silent call button.

Franz had just put his light out when the soft buzzer tripped. His head jerked rapidly to the small security panel, and he signed in disgust. Gabriel had leaned on the button again. This was the second time this week, the fourth in a month. He would have the damned thing moved. He now gave up on the effort to cure Gabriel's carelessness. Tossing the covers from his bed, stood, threw the switch, and started downstairs, wearing only his sandals and robe.

Jerry heard the slap of the sandals a split second before De Hartog reached the door. He backed quickly into the corner leveling the gun, jaws clenched from tension.

"Gabriel, you have pushed the alarm again," Franz said as he stepped through the door.

Jerry had no idea what Franz had said. He didn't speak the language, but he did move forward quick as a cat, clobbering the man behind the ear and catching him as he fell.

Franz woke as he was being tied, saw the man in the black ski mask, and felt nauseous. He started to speak, but the man stuffed a rag in his mouth before he could form a word. For no reason, Franz found himself thinking of his parents. Also, he would need to find new employment.

Jerry expected the consequence of another unexpected meeting would not be good for him. He ripped the gag off the old servant and asked him several questions in French. He found where a few alarms were hidden under rugs, and the location of the switch for the electric eye covering Herr Grousmien's door, and armed with some useful knowledge of the house, he went cautiously upstairs to Grousmien's room. He heard a voice and hesitated at the door. The man was talking to someone on the phone. There was a phone on the hall table and he pondered the odds of being able to listen undetected but dismissed the idea as too dangerous. One side of the conversation would do. He cut the switch for the electric eye and put his ear to the door.

"How long ago did the break-in occur?" Grousmien was asking. There was a pause. "Yes, I want to know anything that you learn from the man. It seems that something quite strange is taking place and it is being kept from us by security."

There was another silence and again Jerry wished that he could hear the other half of the conversation.

"Yes, I agree. The group's quarterly conference is in seven weeks. We will put a few very direct questions to security then. I agree with you, Robert, there have been too many problems this quarter. That's correct; the expenditure in security section is up three hundred percent. Yes, I agree, Robert. Yes, do put Schmitt on."

The conversation then broke into Dutch or German. The group, Jerry thought, grimacing with elation; the invisible thing he'd hunted now had a name. He was so excited that he wanted to pound the wall and restraining the emotion caused the feeling of butterflies to fill his stomach, and he waited while the man continued to talk. Suddenly the conversation was in French again.

"The man is an American for sure then. Yes, yes, I understand. Karl has ordered this himself; you say. Well, we'll demand a full explanation from Van Riebeeck at the meeting. Thank you, Robert. Yes, I will see you at Vila Bon Sabreur. Bon soir."

128

Jerry heard the minuscule click of the phone being hung up and stepped into the room. Grousmien had his back to the door, bending over a briefcase, as Jerry entered the room. Choosing a black folder, he was straightening up when the door was latched. He spun, taking two steps backward, and stumbled into a chair, looking somewhat ridiculous.

Bon soir, Herr Dr. Grousmien," Jerry said softly from behind the pistol. "I bring you greetings from Herr Braun, in Zurich."

Grousmien recovered from his start almost instantly. His reply somewhat surprised Jerry.

"I am perfectly sure that you haven't gone to all this trouble to stop by for a nightcap. But perhaps I can offer you one. I suddenly feel the need for a drink myself, ah - -, your name, sir?"

The name is not relevant to our discussion, Herr Doctor," said Jerry, "nor is the drink."

"If I may ask, sir, is this to be an interview or an assassination, and if the latter, would you accept a sum, exceeding your present fee -- to forget your duty that is? In fact," Grousmien added, "I'm in no position to be penurious, you might as well name your price."

"Sure, Herr Doctor," Jerry said, outwardly pleasant. "Someone with your group had a woman murdered, my wife. They beat her head in and shoved her off a cliff in Africa. My price --- give me back her life and I'll allow you yours. If you can't meet my price, well, I'm sorry."

"Surely you're joking," Grousmien said, looking unsure for the first time.

"I see nothing funny in my negotiation. You see, my personal fortune amounts to some two hundred million dollars. I have, in fact, spent close to seven million dollars just to bring about this conversation," Jerry said, watching the old man wince as he began to comprehend the true nature of the situation. "You see, I might have had this taken care of, but I deemed it much more satisfying to attend to it myself. I did hear that one of my hired technicians has stumbled into your hands. That's unfortunate. It might cost me a few hours' time to replace him."

Grousmien's courage returned to him. If the maniac intended to kill him, it was as good as done, fait accompli. He would not beg.

"You're a corpse, Herr Grousmien. The question is, do you wish to die quickly or slowly?" Before Grousmien could answer there was a soft pop and a bullet tore into his left foot, doubling him with pain. One of Grousmien's hands clutched the hardwood arm of his chair, and Jerry brought a heavy paperweight down, crushing his fingers.

Fear and agony filled the old man's eyes. He looked up in time to see Jerry's trigger finger contract a second time and he screamed as the bullet tore into his knee.

"Mercy, Mon Dieu," he rasped, almost unable to form words with his pain.

"I want the name of all parties in the group, Herr Grousmien," Jerry said, bending to apply a tourniquet. "Otherwise, we will use more subtle methods of persuasion, some of which, according to Herr Braun, you developed during the last war Doctor."

The old man spit in Jerry's face, but he just smiled and wiped it off. "Shit," he thought, feeling sick inside, he was going to have to go through all this again.

It took five minutes to break the old man. What he produced was a ledger the size and thickness of a phone book. Jerry read the names, nearly fifty from the list of principals in disbelief, then pushed the ledger inside his sweater. He was awed by some of the names; they included individuals from a dozen countries, national leaders, prominent men known for lifelong political involvement; men whose fortunes had been in existence long before they were born; men far more prominent than Herr Grousmien, who had personally controlled unhealthy amounts of the world's diamond interests.

Jerry was clear of the estate within fifteen minutes and was still finding it difficult to comprehend the prominence of the individuals listed in the book. Some had to be among the great hypocrites of all time. Stunned by what he learned; he was becoming uncertain for the first time -- no longer optimistic that it would be possible to complete what he had begun.

On his arrival at the International Airport, he began to fear for more than his plans. He could see before he reached the hangar that the Lear Jet was gone and the area was full of police. He gunned the big motorcycle past the hangar and up to the passenger terminal parking area. He put a quick call through to Boston, then purchased a ticket for a Lufthansa flight to London, connecting with a 0300 Pan American flight to New York's JFK Airport. He would handle his business in the East and get back to Denver.

The mental reference to Denver made him think of Nicole again and he cursed himself for this was no time to be forming attachments.

On the London to New York leg, he finally managed to get some sleep.

14

We all of us live too much in a circle.
B. Disraeli

Nov. 15, 1977
4:00 A.M.

From: *Chief Special Security Group*
To: *Security Director*
Subject: *Code ADROIT*

Check on Texidron Corp. shows aircraft was in use between Brazil and United States, at times it was also recorded in Europe and Africa. We have put together a list of all American Aircraft of the type in question not accounted for during the time period July 1, Nov. 13. List is enclosed. There are forty possibilities. The aircraft in question was at Zurich for ten days. It departed at 2200, Nov. 12. Destination, Amsterdam.

Checks of crew and all passengers listed to date has proved futile. No persons answering to those names could have been involved. It must be assumed that false identification was used. These leads are blind and have been discontinued.

Two subjects mentioned in the last report are at this time in Amsterdam having arrived on the 12th from Brussels. I might also add that Herr Braun was in Brussels on the 12th. We suggest a follow up of all parties concerned in Amsterdam.

Evidence has come to light in the last few hours of computer thefts at six different locations. A check of customs records show a John Aims in four of the locations at times of data thefts. This man has also turned out to be untraceable. ID is false, but he, as most of the other parties involved, is believed to be American.

To summarize; this seems to be a very small, but well-organized group. We need a trace on one party to go further. Even the motive eludes us at this time.

Yours respectfully,
Adrien Baptiste

It was 10:00 p.m. on the thirteenth when Rudolf Wagner put a call through to Director Van Riebeeck from Amsterdam. He had questioned the man caught in the secure area of the Trans-Deutschland office, but produced only a few useful facts.

"His name is Dennis Webber," Wagner said, "He's a professional second story man, entry specialist, nationality, American. He was recommended to his present employer by a party in Newport, Rhode Island, United States. Man's name is Leonard Kratz. He has never met his employer but knows him by the name of Best. His work was paid for through a numbered account. The materials he and his partner stole were shipped to various points in the United States. His only contact was a phone booth where he was to wait for a call at a prearranged time in case of a problem. We were waiting on time for the call, but the other hung up. We did get a trace to Denver, Colorado, United States. That call was also made from a pay phone."

"Give me a rundown on the plane's crew," Van Riebeeck said, placing a second tape in his phone recorder, and smiling to himself at the turn of events.

"There is no information on the plane or crew Sir," Wagner apologized, while waiting for the storm to burst about him.

"What do you mean no information?" Van Riebeeck hissed.

"One of our men was killed and two put under fire while attempting to gas the plane's crew. The aircraft took off right down the airport's north taxi-way, nearly causing two mid-air collisions before it cleared traffic," Wagner said.

"I told you not to underestimate these men, Rudi! I told you this twice!" Van Riebeeck said. "What of the other American?"

"We have personnel at all transportation points, but there has been no sign of him. We have only a general description but perhaps we will be fortunate sir."

"Notify Dr. Grousmien's house guards to take extra precautions and you will call me if anything further develops," Van Riebeeck said, hanging up the phone.

He was being undermined by ineptitude, but where was one to find really efficient men anymore? A British Prime Minister to Queen Victoria had said, 'It is difficult to find very many good anything.' 'He was quite correct,' Van Riebeeck thought deciding he must handle this himself. He first called his personal chief back to the office. By midnight he had his choice of fifty men either known to, or employed by, Euro Security Systems. He chose ten names and five alternates: some were ex-police; some were mercenary or regular army types; all spoke English, and all were efficient. He gave his selections to Myers with instructions for ten of them to be at the Conrad Hilton in New York by 2:00 p.m. tomorrow, Brussels time.

His next call was to Adrien Baptiste, who was asleep at his apartment. He gave him the information from Amsterdam and told him to be in touch with him in New York in the morning. He would please provide any background necessary on a Leonard Kratz of Newport, Rhode Island. His secretary booked a flight for him to London, and a connecting 3:00 a.m. flight to JFK New York with Pan American.

Exhausted, he slept thru the entire flight as did most of the other passengers. Arriving at pre-dawn, he checked in at the Hilton, then called Baptiste, taking off his jacket and tie as the call was put through.

"What do you have for me Adrien?" he asked when Baptiste answered.

"We have a good start and are making progress along an interesting line."

The young man spoke in a crisp voice that eased some of Van Riebeek's discomfort at being away from the center of power. This was like that damned Renard thing all over he told himself, only a hundred times worse.

"Continue, Adrien."

"The subject, Leonard Kratz, is connected with organized crime in the Northeastern United States. He provides a personal service, a brokerage if you will, for the syndicate, very efficient and quite expensive. For this service he receives a prearranged fee for each man he puts a customer in line with, as well as a percentage of the technician's fee. For providing this invaluable service, he is under the protection of the syndicate, of course."

"If we have him then, we have the bastards," Van Riebeeck swore in good humor, pounding the desk next to his bed.

"If you had mentioned the name to Myer last night, he might have given you the same rundown. He is in fact, my main source of information. David has in fact used Katz's service on three occasions. He is quite discreet though, moreover Myer has informed me that he does not pass along the names of clients."

"I do not intend to ask Mr. Kratz in a friendly manner more than one time," Van Riebeeck said. He copied down the man's address, list of habits, friends, and other pertinent information, then hung up the phone. He had arranged for cars, weapons, and made an appointment with Kratz for late afternoon, before he received the second call from Baptiste.

His breakfast had just been brought in on a cart and he was spreading jam on a second roll while chewing the first, when the phone rang.

"Yes," he answered.

"Dr. Grousmien was tortured and murdered last night," Baptiste said.

Van Riebeeck choked, spitting bits of roll all over the floor, and upset his tray, "Dead?" he gasped, struggling to his feet. "What time? Where were the guards?"

"Six guard dogs were killed and the night staff, including Franz De Hartog were bound and gagged. Only one of the men was seen, and all escaped without surveillance, sir. We have nothing."

"My God Adrien, if you knew Grousmien's position, what they might know. Let me know of any developments; I must think," he said and hung up on Baptiste again.

Van Riebeeck had heard the reading of his own death warrant. Grousmien was for this two-year period treasurer for the group. He was a man with numerous friends and a fortune amounting to over $400,000,000.00, clear. The death would eventually be blamed on Van Riebeeck, but to save himself he could not understand what motive his opponents had. It seemed so far that they wanted only to know and would kill anyone to gain mere handfuls of facts. But why?

He was so frustrated and tense he couldn't think. He called room service and asked to have his tray removed. When the bellhop arrived, he gave him a fifty-dollar bill and told him he would like the company of a lady, also, if he was pleased and she arrived within thirty minutes, he would have another fifty.

When the first of his team arrived at eight thirty a.m., Van Riebeek's tension had succumbed to the ministrations of a small redhead from the Lower East Side, leaving him at least able to reason intelligibly again. He gave them their instructions and by mid-morning was on his way to Newport. Traffic was unacceptable.

***

Jerry's first act on arriving in New York had been to arrange replacements for the men he had lost in Amsterdam. He didn't know what he was going to do yet, but he might need to get into some place with a lock on it in the near future, moreover he'd need new ID's.

He caught a few hours' sleep and was at the library when it opened. He found a picture of the Villa Bon Sabreur in a book of the 19th century estates of Luxemburg. He researched; the country, the parish, the local villages, and the estate itself over the next few hours. Lunch was from a hot-dog cart on the way to the Federal bookstore in central Manhattan, where he purchased topographical survey maps of the entire area. Satisfied, he caught a taxi to the airport and a afternoon. flight to Boston.

The more he studied the material on Bon Sabreur and pondered the problem, the more hopeless it looked. It

138

was a pseudo castle with a moat, draw bridge and the whole bit. He could think of no way to handle it. An assault force could drop in, but that was ridiculous. Also, there was the computer bank in Brussels along with microfilm records in a nearby bank vault to consider. If he was going to make a complete sweep he would have to destroy all central records as well as the corporate heads. That would cause a chaotic situation from which they could not recover. He knew there would only be one chance to get them all at once. Forty of the world's most financially powerful men. Cunning, ruthless, successful, but he might destroy them and their power structure because they didn't realize he existed. But I know what I'm up against and I have neither room for mistakes nor time to waste, he told himself.

He'd figure it out. In a few days he'd begin planning the last phase of his campaign, his war. There would be a solution; he would find it and he would execute it on January 4th. Too much had happened not to succeed. I can do it, he convinced himself. I won't fail now.

***

"What's this all about?" Carlo asked, looking from face to face.

The men who had beat up his bodyguards and hauled him out of his own bed, remained insensate to him, staring blankly and grimly ahead.

"God damit, what's going on?" Carlo yelled angrily after a few more minutes of silence.

"You obviously have all the answers Mr. Marrinini, or our employer wouldn't have arranged to meet you," the driver said, lapsing back into silence.

Memories of several shady deals eased into Carlo's mind and all of them included small indiscretions that could have upset some of the big boys. Well, maybe one or two weren't so small, but he was sure none of the big boys had ever picked up on them, besides he was damned big himself now. Something wasn't right; this wasn't a normal setup. Thirty years he'd been in the rackets and he knew the score. He knew what happens when you went for a ride, but why? Cold chills ran up his back and of all times he needed to take a leak. "Jesus," he muttered over and over. Who in the hell was crazy enough to pull this stunt?

The office building was a small one in Weymouth. Most of the offices were empty although no one would have been around at that time of the morning anyway. They encountered no one in the halls and the quiet frightened Carlo. They entered an office where two other men were waiting. One punched the intercom and said, "They're here Sir."

"Ask him in," a powerfully strong accented voice answered.

They all have accents, Carlo thought as he was guided through the door; that and he didn't recognize a face in the bunch; they were not only total strangers, they were foreigners. A big square faced man was sitting behind a desk in the inner office. He had a high forehead, thinning blond white hair, and pale almost colorless blue eyes. He very casually motioned Carlo to a seat opposite him and lit a pipe he had been filling.

Van Riebeek's face furrowed deeply as he puffed on the pipe, then relaxed in satisfaction only to rivet abruptly on Carlo.

"Mr. Marrinini," he said, his eyes becoming almost a shade of magenta, "I'm very sorry to have torn you from home and hearth at this hour, but you are a part of a difficult situation. I will be brief. Why did you hire a Dennis Webber and several others to steal information from companies in Europe and Africa; why did you arrange for the assassination of a number of officers of those companies; moreover, who are your accomplices in these activities?"

"I don't know what you're talking about," Carlo blurted, "Really." These guys must be some kind of foreign cops. Somebody had got their wires crossed, he thought.

Van Riebeeck smiled and began digging through some papers in front of him. He selected one and passed it to Carlo.

"Mr. Kratz was good enough to produce this list. He also mentioned your name in reference to it. It seems that these men were recommended to you and one of them, a Mr. Webber, was caught by our people while at work. He has worked for only one person since the list was given to you. Why are you lying, Mr. Marrinini?" Van Riebeeck hissed, slimming the heel of his hand down on the desk.

"Lenny gave you my name?", an absolutely incredulous tone in his voice.

"Not until he suffered a badly dislocated shoulder. I would expect it will throw his golf game off for a short period of time. There are times that a taciturn nature can cause a great deal of discomfort. Do we understand each other, Mr. Marrinini?"

Carlo nodded. If these guys could get to Lenny, they could get to anybody; that and he knew who they wanted. This must be the outfit Capoli had been messing with. Jerry was a good kid. Sure, he liked him but not enough to take his raps.

"Jerry Capoli," Carlo said. "He came to me a few months back and wanted names for a list of skills. I got them and twenty-five grand for my trouble. Another twenty-five for Kratz. All I did was pass Capoli the list and bank my money."

"Capoli, who is Capoli?" Van Riebeeck asked. Carlo told him. Thirty minutes later, Carlo was on his way home and Van Riebeeck was putting through a call to Adrien Baptiste. Industrial spying, the concept seemed ridiculous but it could be possible, though more likely a mere cover story to ease Marrinini's apprehension or curiosity. Jerry Capoli or Jerry Carlton. It was the third name he had worked on in twenty-four hours. The more he learned the less he knew. "Something must open up soon," he thought. There was a limit to the blinds an organization could use to cover itself. Time was against him, though, and to hurry was tantamount to failure. Van Riebeeck had never failed at anything, and he reminded himself of this fact as his Brussels office answered.

142

15

Disadvantages:
"It I difficult to distinguish the insurgent from the
friendly populace in a guerrilla war. To avoid
an ambush and stay alive one must, look for the
little things or kill everyone."
                              From: F.M. 25-79

Jerry saw them there, saw them long before he suspected
anything was wrong, and it was wrong. Only after he
noticed the electrician at the rear of the printer's shop did
the realization of something odd strike him. "My God am I
stupid," he thought, turning abruptly into a dress shop. He
tugged at the pistol under his jacket as two men begin to
walk rapidly his direction and he looked for the rear exit.
The gun was in his hand now and a girl behind the counter
was backing away from him with an expression of fear
transforming her face.

    The guy with the cigar, had spotted Capoli
immediately. He had not done anything suspect, just
continued pitching coins against the wall with his partner,

waiting for Capoli to reach the door of the print shop. They were to take him, not kill him. When Capoli ducked into the dress shop, he knew somehow, they had blown it for his man had stopped short and fled. This unlikely situation caused him to abandon his original line of action for a second plan. He waved his partner toward the end of the street where he could cover the back of the store and moved toward the front. They would have to do this very quickly and shoot only to cripple. He was a veteran of such actions, and was as usual, both confident and frightened. A silenced 3.80 automatic was in his right hand, tucked under his jacket as he neared the front of the shop. Jerry saw the man going for the end of the street at a run. The electrician running toward the other corner. The alley was out. He took a deep breath and ran back out the front.

The man with the cigar, sensed rather than heard the scuff of Jerry's feet in the archway and started to bring up his pistol. They saw each other at the same moment, both firing. He felt a bullet blow by his cheek and fired from the hip. Capoli dove between two parked cars as his second shot smashed a headlight. A silenced pistol is not the least clumsy weapon to fire and spitting out his cigar, he cursed it as he ran toward the front of the car.

Jerry hit the ground between the cars and rolled under the rear of the larger one face up. He aimed between his legs at the running feet and fired. A bullet smashed the man's ankle, pitching him to the pavement; a second caught him in the throat. He gurgled, trying to breath and fight off the shock before he passed out. Jerry was out from under the car and running for his life within a second.

He ran three blocks, before he realized he had been grazed across the back of the left thigh. A man running with a gun in his hand and a blood-soaked left leg is not the least conspicuous sight on a city street. "Don't panic. Get hold of yourself. You just made a stupid mistake; don't make any more," he thought. "Get off the street, then get out of Boston." Underestimate an enemy and he'll kill you. He'd been taught that, so why had he been screwing up? He slowed to a walk tucking the pistol under his jacket. A block further he heard sirens, and wiping the gun clean, dropped it into a storm sewer, then hailed a cab and went to his hotel. Get a car, he thought, and drive at least as far as Albany, New York, then fly to Denver. If they were on Jerry Capa, they were hot. He wasn't sure if they could make a quick connection between his old identity and his present one, but who could tell? Who would have figured they would connect Webber to Carlo and Carlo to himself in 36 hours, plus stake out his Boston contacts? They must really be putting on the pressure with Braun and Grousmien dead.

The thought of Grousmien reminded him of something in the conversation he had overheard. He had been so excited by the other information he had gotten that he had damned near forgotten part of what he had heard. Grousmien had been suspect of the group's security force. Jerry pounded his head trying to recall the name of the head of security. He went over the conversation in his mind several times, writing down what

Grousmien had said. Finally, the phrase came to him, "We'll demand a full explanation from Karl Van Riebeeck at the meeting." Karl Van Riebeeck, Grousmien had said.

Jerry wrote the name down, stuffed it into his wallet, then changed into a fresh suit. What would happen to a man, who made a serious mistake in Van Riebeek's position, Jerry asked himself? If a number of blunders were made, he would be out of a job and knowing what he must, he would be killed rather than simply discharged. He must be playing the whole thing down. Keeping the facts to himself and working around the clock to save his own ass.

Jerry left the hotel by the side door, through a coffee shop. The graze on his leg was bound with a torn sheet and had stopped bleeding but he limped slightly. What if he could get Van Riebeek first, he wondered; would that buy time? He would consider that later. At a 5 & 10 Jerry bought a pair of gloves, then walked to a used car lot on West 34 Street. He looked at several cars but showed interest in a '72 Mustang. The salesman asked him if he wanted to take it for a spin. Jerry drove three blocks, removed the price tag, then pulled into another lot where he looked at station wagons.

He told the owner he would like to show one of his '76 Olds wagons to his wife. Could he leave his car and drive the station wagon home to see what his wife thought? Five hours later he left the stolen wagon at the Albany airport.

He caught a Northwest flight to Cheyenne, Wyoming, where he rented a car. At this point, the two-hour drive to Denver was prudent. They had a name and a picture now and he couldn't take any chances. Look at Henri Renard! He had been killed within twenty hours, at a distance of over a thousand miles from the center of a search pattern and in the middle of a busy airport. Jerry drove and mulled over a hundred possibilities, and a hundred gambits.

***

"Good morning, sir," Van Riebeeck greeted, "What do you have to say concerning the death of Dr. Grousmien?" asked a precise voice on the other end of the line.

"It seems to lead to an organization involved in industrial espionage, sir; based in Europe but staffed by Americans. We have the name of one of the key men. Operatives are in the process of locating him at the present time. I expect to terminate the entire incident within the week, sir."

"Very well, Karl. I will expect a full report on the subject at termination. To move on now, explain the statements as of November 12 -- concerning the Rhodesian operation and our present funding in Angola -- explain please."

"I can be no more explicit than I was in the report, sir. Angola must be written off at present. The Communists have gained too much too fast. We can affect them over a period of time but have no real control over any part of the situation now. Myself and my field chief in the area believe any financial expansion into the area at this time would be nearly impossible for us to protect. He believes that the situation will hit low points within 18 months and I concur. By then, all will be in ruin. That will be the time to move in if you wish to purchase at bottom. The local power structures should have stabilized by then but it will be a long-term outlook. We will elaborate in our quarterly report at Bon Sabreur, sir."

"I will want a detailed report in three days, Karl! Now, what of the Rhodesian situation? You were rather vague concerning the Umvickwes Chromium Mines. We had planned to control them by February of 1980."

"The directive sent to me by your committee was based on Jason Moya's influence with Nkomo, and since his assassination we've been unable to meet certain objectives. On the other hand, what happened to the influence that was to be exerted by the British and Americans? We have fanned the flames and at any time the specified industries can be wrecked, but who is to keep the Kaffirs from gaining control of the situation, as in Mozambique and Angola? With all due respect, sir, political contacts of such high order are not the responsibility of this section. The delays and problems are not entirely our fault."

"I am beginning to think Security is without responsibility Director Van Riebeeck," said the precise man.

"We take responsibility when the failing is ours, sir," Van Riebeeck retorted, angry but controlled.

"We will see, Karl. I await your reports."

There was a distinct click and Van Riebeeck smashed the receiver down, wondering, not for the first time, how he might get away with the assassination of James Holms. Nothing seemed to proceed smoothly at the moment. He had literally lost control of himself yesterday at hearing of the escape of the American in Boston. He should have returned to Brussels. If Baptiste did not pick up something new, the man might prove impossible to locate. The man was an enigma. It was as if he had ceased to exist.

He pressed the play switch on his recorder, and listened to the tape on Jerry Carlton, or Capoli, as he had been known to Carlo Marrinini. It was not the first time he had heard it, but when it ran out, he hit rewind and played it back again. The voice was young, but crisp and business like.

Subject born, Brooklyn, N.Y., Feb. 3, 1947. Birth certificate names – Mother: Andrea Carlton, Father: Frank Capoli. Parents unmarried. Mother, alcoholic, died 1950. Father, low level member of syndicate, killed in prison 1960.

Subject was ward of State, passed through several foster homes before 1960. Put into State Reform School for two years, 1960-1962, for complicity in a robbery assault.

August 1962 was released to his paternal aunt, Gina de Angelo, and attended school in Boston through 1966. Juvenile records during this period have him listed on suspicion in five assault cases and three cases of auto theft. No convictions.

Subject enrolled Suffolk University, August 26, 1966. Though highly intelligent, he did poorly in basic courses. Low D average in first semester, D+ in second semester. Loss of deferment to low scholastic scoring, he received an induction notice May 1, 1967 and was inducted into the United States Army on June 4, 1967. He formed few relationships during this period and seemed to have had no close friends. Family have not seen him since July of 1966. We are attempting to locate individuals presently to obtain further information.

Subject's military background includes: Airborne and Special Forces training, and twelve months combat experience in Laos 68/69. Discharged at the rank of Staff Sergeant June 4, 1969. Army rates subject as well disciplined, highly intelligent, combat skilled, and efficient.

Inheritance of one Hundred eighty million and control of General Systems of Jersey from Maternal Grandfather May 24, 1969. Present worth estimated at Two Hundred Ten million.

Married 1970, Constance Johnson, OR , United States. Spouse departed Africa on same date as subject and location is presently unknown.

Subject was employed by the United Nations Food and Agriculture Organization from 7/2/72 until 9/5/73 in Dabuta. Transferred to Research and Advisement position in 1973. Last position with F.A.O. Dedougou, Upper Volta. Applied for leave of absence and returned home with wife on 6/9/77.

Subject traveled through: Chad, Nigeria, Niger, Mali, Mauritania, Central African Empire, Zaire, Rhodesia, Uganda, and Zambia between July 4 and August 18.

Subject made all personal, equipment, and identification arrangements on return from the trip. Dropped out of sight on September 3rd. Motivation unknown."

Van Riebeeck punched the stop button. Since yesterday, he had employed three large detective agencies, as well as bringing another 30 of his own people to the United States. A thousand facts had been fed to Euro Securities Computers in the last 24 hours and logic told him that something must unfold. It is impossible for a man to vanish in this age without some record, some trace, and he would find it.

He looked at Carlton's picture again, pondering. He was missing something that was right in front of him. He knew it. His mind was stressed to the point of becoming dis-functional. The man seemed somehow familiar, but he couldn't place him. The whole thing was infuriating, particularly the question of Carlton's motivation. What was the man attempting? He wondered, did he have any close friends or family, perhaps if the other avenues were unproductive.

16

"God hath no wrath like a woman scorned.

When Jerry arrived at the ranch it was nearly 1:00 A.M. Mountain Time and snow had begun to fall. He slipped, getting from the car, and fell on his leg, causing it to start bleeding again. Limping into the house, hungry, exhausted and sore, he went to Nicole's room and switched on the light, waking her.

She sat up in bed, dazzled by the light, afraid for a moment, as if she had awakened from a nightmare. The moment she recognized him, she blurted, "Your aircraft, it was attacked last night in Amsterdam, she blurted. "People answered the phone for the first time; at least one man has been caught. Has someone got careless, or have they guessed what's happening?"

Jerry looked at her for a moment. "He said, "careless, no but someone is certainly aware of our existence, if not our location. Get up, Nicki, and I'll tell you about it while you work on my leg."

She climbed quickly from the bed, following him into the kitchen, where he had already begun to remove his pants. She gasped at the sight of the bandage blackened with blood, fresh blood oozing through and trickling down his leg. There was a first aid kit in one of the cupboards and she pulled it down, opening it on the kitchen table.

"You were shot?" she asked.

"Just a crease. A crease is nothing but I'll admit, painful as hell. I've had worse." He smiled, but the smile did not go as far as his eyes. He stood bent, holding his leg as Nicole, now silent, cut away the bandage. His flesh was feverish and sensitive near the wound; her fingers were cool and firm. Despite the discomfort, there was a sensuality in the way she worked, washed it, applied the new dressing. He found himself looking down the front of her nightgown, as a sudden sense of intumescences darted into his groin. Embarrassed, he tried to put his mind elsewhere.

"They've nailed down my contacts on the East Coast," he said flatly. "Damned near got me too, but I believe we're safe here."

"You mean, they really know who you are," she said, allowing a trace of fear to permeate her voice.

"They have a name and a picture, Nicki, but they don't know who I am. Nobody knows who I am in the real sense."

"Or what," she said with a touch of acid.

"And what's that supposed to mean?" he answered, annoyed.

"I read the papers, the kidnapping. I read what had been done to Braun. He was but a banker, and his family was terrorized. The children will never forget. How many acts of violence and terrorism must I be a party to? I feel unclean, as if I am as bad as they are. I want an end to this," she said, and jerked a last piece of tape against his leg.

"Damn you," Jerry said, restraining his own temper. "Well, we've got an end to it in sight," he said, spitting out the words with a sort of triumph. "Not only do I have a list of names, but I have the nine multi-national corporations involved, and the name of their Security organization. I even know when and where the next meeting is, and I'm going to get every last one of the bastards!"

"That's not possible for one man," she said with disdain. "Not for a man who is known. Besides, it would not solve the problem, by killing them. My father meant to expose them. Let the authorities attend to them. If you have the facts, present them to the widest possible audience, and those involved will be literally torn apart."

Jerry had sunk into a chair to listen as she continued. Her face and voice were full of anger, and passion. Not hot, but cold, like an arctic light flooding, dampening his own passions. He was tired but was fueled by anger. Too much anger to leave it all to others. That would be to leave it to chance.

"But maybe you're right, Nicki," he said, when the tirade ended. "All I've got is names. We'd have to get our hands on every record in every file those outfits have. With enough time, we could put it all together, but if we go after the information in their computer files, they're going to be on us fast, Nicki."

Jerry paused for a moment and gazed straight at her. There was an intensity in the look as he spoke again. "It was too bad about the banker's family but they're going to get over it. As far as the other things I've done, well, there's too much violence in my past. A fight, for me, can't end in a pull-up and a handshake, any more than it could for the people who killed your father. It ends in death. If we can get the information we need, we'll take a crack at turning it over to newspapers and governments simultaneously. If it doesn't work, and I'm still alive, I'll try to destroy them in a more direct fashion -- if that can be done. Everything they do is covered by the sharpest industrial security agency in Europe. Its Euro Secure who arranges their dirty work."

He reached down, began to pull his pants back on, stood and zipped the front. Nicole was still standing rooted in the same spot. Now her face was unmistakably softer, some of the earlier tension gone. He felt an almost unbearable loneliness sweep over him, and another twinge of desire, but he turned from her, opening the refrigerator.

"Wait," she said, "I'll make you something. Go in the living room and rest." She made a light meal and put it on the dining room table. Nicole found him on the couch snoring peacefully. She watched him sleep for a moment, then carefully bent, and woke him with a shake of his foot. They talked while they ate.

He told her what he had learned in the last ten days in detail, and they discussed the possible chances of being found at the ranch. "At any rate," he said, "we're going to spend the next few days preparing to steal their computer records, and then get out of here."

"But why leave? You just said we were very secure here."

Jerry smiled and restrained a nervous laugh. "We aren't safe anywhere, Nicki. No matter what, unless every man on that list, and a lot that aren't, dies, we're as good as dead. Even if what we do is a hundred percent successful, we aren't safe."

"It's a large world. People can vanish. Those with assets can vanish completely."

Jerry took a deep breath; the scent of perfume and the nearness of Nicole's body were making the conversation difficult. "Let's hope you're right, because after we poke around in Euro Securer's computer center, and they've had more time to research my recent history, we're going to need to disappear. At least until we get the information out, or January 4th."

She nodded, "Yes." Her voice became very soft. "And what do we do after?"

"We," Jerry said, yawning, "go to bed and worry about that if we're still alive after."

"That is the first pleasant suggestion you've made this evening," she said, smiling, and leaning quickly over the table, kissed him.

"Hey, I meant to our own beds," Jerry said, trying to lean back away from her.

The expression that came across her face was pure fury. She pushed him backwards causing his chair to turn over, dumping him painfully on the floor.

"Oh!" she yelled, picking up a bowl. "I forgot your precious advantages of being alone."

The bowl struck Jerry in the side of the head covering his face with shrimp Creole. He had just managed to crawl clear of the chair when the half gallon carton of milk hit him.

"Cut it out, Goddammit," he cursed, trying to rub the shrimp sauce out of his eyes.

"Oh, feeling a bit bristly now," she cried, letting fly with a coffee cup. "You're letting yourself be reached emotionally, Mr. Carlton. Temper, temper," she taunted, reaching for a plate.

Jerry could see out of one burning, tearing eye and lunged at her feet as the plate sailed over his head. She screamed in rage and fell on top of him, scratching and kicking. One of her knees hit him square in the face, giving him a nosebleed.

"Goddammit, Nicki, calm down," he swore, rolling across her, managing to get control of one of her arms. "I'm sorry."

"Sorry for me or yourself, you're a selfish pig?" she hissed vehemently. "You have no concern for other people's feelings," she said, trying to get a clear swing at his face with her free arm.

"Okay, you win," he groaned, catching her other wrist. Blood, shrimp sauce and all, he kissed her until she stopped struggling. "Do you want a long engagement or short?" he asked a few moments later.

"We may not live to see long so, short," she said simply, and began to laugh at the mess she'd made of him. "What a ridiculous way to become engaged," she thought.

***

November 17, 1977

1:00

P.M.
EURO SECU:
From: Chief, Special Security Group
To: Director
Subject: Code, ADROIT

    We have connected a great deal in the past eight hours. Key factor is individual Jerry Carlton, listed on report received this branch yesterday.

    He has necessary financing education and experience to have carried out operations.

Subjects dealings with Carlo Marrinini.

Subject's presence in two of our operational areas.

Subject's possible acquaintance with one or more of our operations in Central Africa.

Cash flows of over 7 million from his accounts during the last few months.

Subject's company has not used one of it's aircraft for the last 85 days. Aircraft is a Lear Jet, of type involved in all operations.

Total disappearance of Carlton and wife and their failure to follow normal behavior pattern is highly suspect.

All evidence ties his center of operation to Denver, Colorado. Also, we might add that Denver is the location of a computer company in which he holds the controlling stock.   We suggest that all investigations be directed toward Carlton and the Denver area. We await further data.

Yours respectfully,

Adrien Baptiste

Van Riebeeck sat tapping his pen against his head, then reached out and circled a section of the report. He flipped the switch on his intercom and ordered several files brought to him. When they arrived, he flipped through various reports, pausing briefly to jot down times and dates. He pulled a packet of four photos from the Renard file and studied them carefully. Henri Renard was short and slightly built with reddish brown hair and a boyish face. Another photo taken by the police was of his corpse. Van Riebeeck had never seen the face before. Suspicion tugged at him. Strange, he thought, reaching for the phone. He dialed quickly and waited for an answer.

"Baptiste here."

"Adrien, a number of things, and quickly. I want customs checks made for the dates 6/14/77 through 6/20/77. I wish to know how and when Henri Renard left Upper Volta and with whom. Secondly, how and when Jerry Carlton and his wife left Upper Volta. I want the arrival and departure times in Dakar and whatever photographs are available of Carlton and Mrs. Carlton.

"We should be able to give you a readout within the hour, sir," Baptiste said. "We recorded all customs date beginning 6/1/77 at the beginning of Adroit. I'll try and get the photos and teletype and be back with you presently."

"Bring me the information personally, Adrien," Van Riebeeck said and hung up. Walking to the window, Van Riebeeck raised slowly up and down on the balls of his feet, waiting and watching the traffic below.

***

Jerry awoke early, but lay thinking for some time. Nicole snuggled against him in her sleep causing a lingering sensation to run through him. A life with her would not be the comfortable easygoing existence he had with Connie. Nicki did nothing in half measures, nor could she be put off or even controlled once she had made up her mind. It would be exciting, he mused, like living in a tiger's den or on top of a live bomb.

She was the first person in his life that he had not been able to keep at arms length. Even with Connie he had been able to maintain some distance, but Nicole would not allow it. She pierced every guard he put up, and to make matters worse, she could see right through every subterfuge he attempted. He leaned over and kissed her lightly. Nothing is going to happen to this one, he swore to himself, as she responded sleepily to his kiss.

"Umm, is it late, Amie?"

"Almost noon, Nicki."

"Umm, what a lovely way to wake," she murmured luxuriantly stretching. Rolling over, she nuzzled his chest. "Say it again bien Amie."

"Say what?"

"How much you love me."

"Mildly," he said, smirking, then let out a startled scream as she tore a patch of hair out of his chest with her teeth.

Jerry hugged her head against his side, squirming. "I love you lots. I'd swim the sea, eat worms," he swore.

"Say it nice, darling," she giggled, twisting a patch of hair on his stomach between her thumb and forefinger, making him pronounce the words with the proper inflection. Her green eyes met his mischievously, and she hugged herself against him again, satisfied that his training was progressing properly.

It was nearly an hour before they got around to lunch, but over lunch Nicole became all business. They discussed which data they would attempt to pull from the group's computer and in what order. The prime pieces of information would be the construction and security blueprints for Bon Sabreur and the computer center itself. Next, they would try for complete personnel records. Last would be the financial records.

"How long will it take them to trace the data outflow?" Jerry asked.

She gave a small laugh. "How long does it take for ice to melt? This answer depends on the heat, as yours depends on their security and attentiveness."

"If they spot the intrusion instantly, how long will it take to trace the outflow to this teleprocessing terminal?" he asked after a moment.

"Considering that they can intimidate Bell Telephone Corporation, or have influence with it, thirty minutes."

"Jesus Christ!" Jerry swore.

"We have their computer codes. They shouldn't notice a thing. Even if they do catch something, it will take time to check out their own branch offices," she said.

"No, that's gambling, Nicki. We set everything up to leave, then disappear one hour after we begin the readout. We can go over the date in Miami and make arrangements from there."

"When do we begin?" she asked.

"When it's about 9:00 P.M. here it will be 3:00 A.M. in Western Europe. People will be at home, difficult to contact, out of sorts. We do it then. I'm going to charter a helicopter this afternoon and we'll plan on leaving from a spot about four miles from here tonight. Drive out the back way. Fly a few hundred miles to Dodge City, then continue to Florida by car," Jerry smiled, "You ever been a tourist?"

By early afternoon, he'd made arrangements for the helicopter to be delivered to a spot near a vacation home on the far side of the ridge. One of the guards, Allen McIvor, had flown helicopters in Vietnam and Jerry approached him on the question of picking the chartered helicopter up and flying him southeast to Dodge City, Kansas. The rest of the guards were notified that their jobs would terminate at midnight. He paid them off with two weeks' severance pay and then told them to stay outside the fence and on their bellies after nine.

"If somebody tries to get in here tonight, you people will have ten thousand apiece coming. That is, if you keep me alive to pay it," he added with a sardonic half grin.

The men chuckled and went back to work. Jerry began burning papers.

17

"Doom is not always preceded by a crack."

"Paaft!" Van Riebeeck roared as he slung the letter opener across the room. There was a sharp thunk, and Adrien Baptiste sat watching it vibrate from where the blade had driven three inches into the wall.

"A chance in a million, a fluke," Van Riebeeck swore, waving the pictures in his hand. "Who would have ever imagined such a coincidence?" he swore, throwing the pictures onto the desk.

"I don't quite understand Sir," Baptiste said, unsure of the drift things had taken. He realized Carlton must have had some sort of contact with the Renard's, perhaps conspired with them from the beginning, but Van Riebeek's behavior astounded him. There was something more to this than he could grasp at the moment.

"Never mind, never mind Adrien," the director said, composing himself. "For the moment, let us say I have an insight into Mr. Carlton's motives. Also, I commend you for succeeding brilliantly at what I could call a nearly impossible intelligence problem. How long would it take to get me a brief on the Denver, Colorado area, also any of Carlton's' holdings in that area, Adrien?"

"You will receive them within 30 minutes Sir," Baptiste said standing. "By, say five."

"Good," Van Riebeeck said, and switching on his intercom, informed his secretary that the office staff was to remain at work until he ordered otherwise. Also, he would require a charter jet in two hours. He gave her several names and instructed her to have his team on his private line within the hour. A sharp click terminated the one-sided conversation, and he leaned back from his deck to think.

How many individuals in a world population of four billion would have had the intelligence, skills, and personal resources to have done what Carlton had done? What minute percentage would have reacted as rapidly and precisely to such a set of circumstances? The odds against such a thing were one in ten million, he surmised. "So why had this happened to me?" he wondered.

He began to theorize as to what kind of a man this American was; how his mind would work. Van Riebeeck closed his eyes, picturing the dry dusty plateau of Upper Volta and the sight of the jeep crashing downhill. When the man was thrown clear, his first action was to go into the river after his companions. Only after he found them dead did he attempt to escape, Van Riebeeck thought. This was the only mistake he could spot. After his one moment of weakness, he had become flawless in his actions.   Instead of running, he had become the aggressor. His weakness had been his wife.

There had been no report of his companions' deaths to anyone. Not only had there been no report, but certain facts had been covered completely. He had moved in a direct line from the fringe areas to one of the central figures of the group in little more than five months. The man has power, wealth, education, but is an emotional primitive, Van Riebeeck finally decided.   Biblical in his outlook. An eye for an eye. He would wish to destroy not only the figures at the top of the pyramid, but the entire structure.   He would not be naïve enough to expect assistance from society, so he would undertake the task singularly, and violently. Cut off the head and the beast dies.   The group would be more like dealing with the legendary Hydra, only with many more than seven heads.

How would I go about the eradication of over fifty of the world's most powerful figures, Van Riebeeck asked himself? To assassinate them piecemeal, would militate against success for the deaths of the early victims would warn the rest.   To coordinate 42 simultaneous deaths involving persons of the group's stature, would strain the CIA or KGB, he thought.

I would act when they were at one location. Bon Sabreur, on the 4th would present the ideal opportunity, he mused.   For this I would complete information on the complex. Carlton has successfully stolen information from computer banks before. He will contemplate the danger of repeating the action to obtain his information from the only complete source and he will decide that it is a necessary risk. Van Riebeeck opened his eyes, smiling broadly as his phone rang, thinking, 'when he does, I will checkmate him, Personally.'

By 7:00 p.m. European time, Van Riebeeck was on a jet bound for Denver, via New York, and security had a full time monitor on the Brussels computer complex. Eight hours later a phone rang inside a warehouse on Denver's north side. One of several men answered. He picked up the phone, nodded and passed the receiver to Van Riebeeck.

"Someone dialed into the computer by way of an overseas phone line, ten minutes ago, sir. Our contact with Bell says the teleprocessor terminal is registered to a research group. It's located at 6954 Route 89, three miles off Interstate 25. That's fifteen minutes from your location. Out in the sticks."

"Thank you, Van Riebeeck said and hung up. He stood and turned to a short dark man behind a desk. "Make the calls, Harold. Also, be sure the radios are monitored."

Gazing at a map on the desk, Van Riebeeck circled the location, then placed and "X" near the circle. "Rendezvous at this junction in twenty minutes," he ordered. "And be sure each man understands the precariousness of our position if we should fail to perform our assignment with precision this time."

A few minutes later the Director turned to his driver as they were moving on to Interstate 25. "What, may I ask, does 'out in the sticks' mean?"

"Rural area, isolated," the man answered.

"Interesting colloquialism," Van Riebeeck thought.

***

"How long yet, Nicki?"

"The last of it's coming through, maybe five minutes."

"It better be. We must have 200 pounds of paper here already."

"How long has it been now?" she asked.

"Forty-five minutes," he said, placing another stack of computer printout in a box. "I put the security and personal stuff in that briefcase. We'll take it along. The rest of it's too bulky. I'm going to have Mike ship it."

There was a sudden silence as the machine stopped clattering out its ten lines a second.

"That's the last of it, darling," Nicole said, tearing out the last sheet.

"Okay! I'll give Mike a call and we'll get these things loaded," Jerry said, climbing the stairs.

He pressed the intercom button labeled garage, and called, "Hey, Mike." He repeated the call after a moment, still getting no answer. His eyebrows knitted and he moved slowly across the darkened room to the window. He looked out just in time to see one of the Dobermans begin to stagger in a tight circle and fall, twitching about 50 feet from the house.

Although his eyes saw, his mind didn't register at once. It was the sight of Mike crawling out of the garage, retching that brought the realization to him. "My God," he said out loud, "gas." Fear clutched at him and he began to run for the basement stairway. He was halfway down the stairway shouting to Nicki to get into the tunnel when his mind regained control again. Crossing the basement, he jerked the breaker switches, cutting power to the house. The lights went out and the air-conditioning ground to a halt.

"What's wrong?" a touch of anguish and strain accented Nicole's voice.

"They're here and they're using nerve gas. Get in the tunnel and run. I'll catch up. And take the briefcase!"

"But what are you going to do?"

"Shut up and run, goddammit!" he shouted, beginning to turn over the boxes of computer paper. He lit a match, carefully cupped it and put the flame to the paper. In the light of the rapidly burning blaze, he tore paint cans, thinner, cleaning fluids, everything flammable from the shelves, smashing them on the floor or against the stairwell. He could hear the sound of wood splintering someplace upstairs as he plunged into the tunnel.

'That will confuse the issue for a while,' he thought starting into the tunnel. Hate welled up into his throat as he ran, and he fought it back. 'You can't think clearly with your emotions involved. You know that, now calm down,' he prompted himself. First the gas. Gas of that type dissipates quickly. They would have put it out from cylinders upwind of the ranch. Anti-personnel gasses are heavier than air. The tunnel runs uphill and cross wind, so the entrance should be clear of gas. The fire is going to bring a lot of people into the area so they'll get out of here damned fast. 'No, they won't do that,' he thought, 'I wouldn't. To coordinate this thing, they must be using radios. If it were me, I would also cover the roads. They wouldn't be planning on the fire, though. That's going to upset the bastards.'

The mental picture of a frenzied search of the house, with flames rising on all sides, caused him to break out laughing as he ran. He was still laughing when he neared the end of the tunnel.

"Jerry, Jerry. Is that you?" The sound of Nicole's voice sobered him.

"Yes, keep your voice down."

"Are we safe?" There was a shake in her voice and Jerry took hold of her, pulling her body tight against him. The night was cold, and she was shivering already.

"No, but we're not dead either, Nicki. There's a bonfire back there to discourage pursuit, but if somebody is smart, they'll figure we're not in it. It's not hard to spot the area this pipe was laid in, so they're going to be heading this way. We should have a few minutes head start at the least, though."

"Where are we going?"

"Cross country to the helicopter and quick."

"I can't run too well in this skirt," she said looking down. "Too tight," she added.

"Turn," he said and split the side of her skirt. He took the briefcase out of her hand and turned her uphill. "Come on Nicki, we've got four miles to cover."

***

A cold frustration grabbed Van Riebeeck when the conformation of the tunnel was reported. The report that it was free of gas did not help to slow his racing mind. Who would have guessed at nearly a kilometer of escape tunnel, or the man having the presence of mind to block it by burning down a house. This time he didn't censure himself for Carlton's escape. The man was incredibly cunning. This was the first instance that Van Riebeeck could remember ever having judged another man to be his equal. He would have to begin thinking in an entirely different manner to deal with him.

To start with, there would not be enough time to get men organized and moving into the woods. Local police will be here very soon. It would be ridiculous to attempt a night pursuit of that man in a forest anyway, so he had ordered his men to pull out. They would cover transportation centers and hope.

"Hope," Van Riebeeck snorted. "What a futile word."

State Police and fire fighters descended on the ranch within minutes of Van Riebeek's departure. They found a number of dead or very sick dogs, eleven armed men in critically ill condition, and a burning building. The story was as big on the eleven o'clock news; almost as big as Sadat's proposed trip to Israel. It was equally as large on the morning edition. Seeing the thing on television frazzled the Dutchman's already frazzled nerves even more. He was in the midst of the most complex series of operations ever attempted by a non-government organization. The culmination of five years of dangerous, costly manipulation.   Fifteen African economies were affected and the next months would be crucial. He hadn't the time to waste on this Carlton.

The group now had control of almost thirty percent of world copper and cobalt. Uranium and tungsten were also being picked up and were scheduled for accelerated expansion in 1979.   The world chromium market was within twenty months of being cornered.

Van Riebeek's job entailed the physical aspects of the campaign. The coordination of incidents. Seeing that no one operational area knew of any ties to another. The events that happened day today, were to fit into the tableau of world events. They sometimes would control the events, sometimes make use of them.

The projected destruction, and flooding of Zaire's cobalt and copper mines in the spring of 1978, would drive the value of other sources up. Cobalt would soar on the world market. Copper, after a few more incidents, would follow.   Profits would allow the purchase of controlling interests in sabotaged properties. The system would be used again in Rhodesia within eighteen months.

Rebels now attack only soft targets. Prices were falling with confidence. Several countries were meddling politically and Van Riebeek's people were hard at work. Within the year the mining industry would come under attack and cease to function. Substantial pressure would fall on the industrial nations to stabilize the Rhodesian political situation, and it would stabilize even if under rebel control. Zambia would be handled in a similar manner.

Blame would be cast everywhere, particularly on American policies in the area, and Soviet backing of the rebels.

The eventual control of 70 percent the free world's industrial raw materials was the long-range goal. The European based cartel, which envisioned and planned the project, had multiple goals. Not only would they make massive profits, but also the monopoly of mineral deposits and production would effectively counter the Arab oil cartel. Inflation would slow on the continent, but soar in the United States, South America, and Japan. The value of the dollar, already battered by the huge oil import deficits, would plummet, again increasing the value of European currencies, and the group's ability to expand. Possibilities were unlimited.

Even if Van Riebeeck could not quite imagine the world corporate government that some of the top people said they were evolving toward, he was realistic enough to see that corporate war already existed. If he was to survive it, he must be free to function, and halfway through the news a possibility occurred to him. Although he didn't have the resources to track Carlton down, the Americans did. So let them do it -- Motivate them. If they considered the man a dangerous criminal, they would hunt him. First, van Riebeeck would link him to the ranch. Then something more creative. He made the necessary calls by nine.

By ten a.m. an APB was issued nationwide. APB on Jerry Carlton. Shortly afterward the FBI entered the search, after anonymous calls leaked information of his involvement in a conspiracy to steal top secret weapons from the Army's Rocky Mountain Arsenal. He was painted as a radical; he was tied to the gassing incident at the ranch; other evidence was planted, and he was well framed.

On his chartered jet eastbound over Lake Superior, Van Riebeeck prepared to get some sleep. 'Let someone locate Carlton; then I will try to have him killed,' he thought. He had begun to formulate a second plan also, for if he couldn't dispose of the American soon, he would have to have a ready plan to save himself. The idea galled him for it would entail giving up much of what he valued. Above all, he was a practical man, though, so he would create options.

Nicole was 60 miles south of Dallas on I-35 when she heard the police APB on Jerry Carlton. She woke him with a quick shake and pulled off the road at the next exit.

"Oh, that's sweet," Jerry muttered under his breath when he was wide awake enough for the full weight of the problem to hit him.

"Is there much danger of our being caught?" Nicole asked, brushing hair from her face.

"Not much, I guess, but it's going to be more difficult to move around. I could hide out in the woods forever, but what good would that do?" They sat in silence for a few minutes before he spoke again. "We're going to get married and go on a honeymoon."

"What?"

"No wait for blood tests or a license in Texas. We can be married in three hours. Then we honeymoon in

Galveston. Rice, marriage license, and all. Perfect cover, and I do love you."

"You had better add that last part," she said. "And who am I to be?"

"How about Mrs. Brubecker?" Jerry asked with a grin. It's the only ID I've got with me. A wig and a mustache might not be a bad idea either.

She sat shaking her head at the absurdity of the situation, smiling herself. "People fall in love with the strangest people, don't they Bien Amie?"

The ceremony was performed north of Houston, and they arrived at the Admiral Hotel in Galveston before mid-night. The following days were spent analyzing the contents of the one briefcase of security material they had managed to save. They discussed and argued the possibilities of gaining access to the other information a second time, finally deciding it was impossible. Nicole was forced to admit any disclosure of the cartel's actions were futile without proof. She had to agree that perhaps Jerry's more direct and violent proposition was all that was left. Studying the security papers on the organization, they began to realize their limited resources might not be enough. It might not be possible.

On the afternoon of the 25th they had dinner at Hill's Seafood Restaurant on the beach. Afterward, they had walked along the surf talking. At a less used and open section of the beach several boys flying Radio Controlled model planes caught his eye. He watched them, totally fascinated for several minutes before telling Nicole what had just occurred to him.

When they checked out of the hotel the next morning, they had the solution to Bon Sabreur. The details could be handled in Florida.

PART III

18

"The best laid plans of mice and men tend to go awry."
-R. Burns

"I'm delighted to hear this, Karl, positively delighted," the precise voice said. "You failed to include projected expenditures, though."

"My financial planning section has hinted at ê3,000,000 quarterly, sir," Van Riebeeck answered.

"Rather a bit steep for a few black radicals, wouldn't you say, Karl?"

"No! You know perfectly well what effect Grousmien's penurious attitudes had on the situation in Mozambique. Any time the outcome is clouded you must back all factions in order to gain leverage within the circle of power. Then we can control the outcome and insure being on the winning side."

"The cost factor will need further discussion, Karl."

"Rubbish," Van Riebeeck spat. "You pay for technical expertise in war; then you argue with it. You get only what you are willing to pay for; moreover, events do not await discussions. Rhodesia will cost ê1,000,000 a month."

"Can you itemize?"

"Starting this month, we plan to support the more moderate groups. We will back them with ê5,000,000. ê3000,000 will go to specialists in all organizations, and ê2,000,000 to combined rebel groups. The decision to back a moderate black government has been handled by channeling large amounts to Bishop Muzowera's party. We will support a merger of Smith's government and the moderates, by funding both, of course. Z.A.P.U. and Z.A.N.U. will receive only token amounts this quarter. Plans to upset their growth and training schedule have been initiated. The first was through information injected into the government last month at a cost of ê20,000. The result was the raid into Mozambique yesterday."

"Yes, 1,200 dead I hear, quite successful, Van Riebeeck, if you can maintain the level of pressure."

"The real heat-up will begin in late 1978, sir, on schedule. The blueprints are already drawn. I might add that we have also put sixty more trained men into the Katangan force for next May's operation in Zaire. Nobody will be able to control that invasion once it starts."

"That's as brief as I can be. I haven't really the paperwork at present, Sir. Grenchman's itemized report should reach your committee in the morning," Van Riebeeck said.

"Thank you, Karl. I'll lend my support, but I will also expect concrete results," the voice said.

"Mr. Holms, one matter I must continue to press. If members of our cartel cannot influence a hands-off policy among the large powers, we will lose control rapidly. I keep reminding myself of Angola," Van Riebeeck grumbled.

"Now, now, Karl, all is well in hand, at present. By the way, what was the outcome of the Grousmien matter?" Holms asked.

"It came to nothing. A strange set of circumstances, but no threat. The man behind the thing was an American, J. Norland Carlton. He was somehow tied up in the thefts of industrial and military secrets. Our people are still digging to place Grousmien's position in the muddle but there seems to be no connection to the group, and Mr. Carlton is now being sought by several agencies in his own country."

"Interesting, Karl," Holms said. "I would like to have a brief on it, when all the facts are known."

Van Riebeeck smiled to himself and scribbled a memo. All the facts would never be known, on this one, he promised himself.

They terminated the conversation on a more cordial note for a change. Van Riebeeck put down the receiver and glanced at his calendar again. November 27th already, and no sign of Carlton. 'If he could not be found within thirty-four more days," Van Riebeek thought, "we will have to intercept him at Bon Sabreur.' It would be difficult. Security would have to be superb, absolutely perfect. The area was guarded by hidden cameras now; however, he would add electronic sensors and anti-personnel radar.

Rising from his desk, he walked to a map at the south side of his office. He studied it again, making several small changes with a grease pencil. He would have Marriot come up after lunch and pick holes in the defenses. The basic plan would stand, though. Three rings of men: one at 500 meters, one at 1 kilometer, one at 5 kilometers. The outer line would watch; the second line would allow passage; the 500-meter circle lets nothing pass. Let the man come within 500 meters and trip the silent alarms. He wouldn't get back out.

No sense in waiting until the last minute to set the screen up. Tomorrow would be good. *Prepare in advance, and never engage with an enemy whose strength and disposition you don't know.* These were two of the golden rules of the military branch Carlton had been part of. Wise rules for any undertaking.

Carlton would most likely arrive early to check the area out; he would want to be well prepared. He might not expect strong security a week ahead of time, so it would be placed ahead of time. The best of chances for trapping him were well before the 4th -- As long as he played true to form he could be handled -- any known quantity could be handled.

***

Eleven fifty a.m., Charter Flight 412 received clearance to land and banking out of the traffic pattern, it began its final approach. The old Super Constellation lumbered out of the misty winter sky onto the south runway of Glasgow's airport, blowing two tires on the second bounce and nearly skidding from the runway before the pilot regained control.

Rafferty taxied toward the cargo terminal visibly shaken. His co-pilot and navigator could see he was nervous but accounted it to the poor visibility and a rough landing. Rafferty knew better. Although he had been checked out on the Connie's controls by the previous owner, he had never flown her. In fact, he had never flown a four-engine plane before today and considering the weather, the landing had been a little more difficult than he had anticipated.

At customs, he presented the plane's papers and his own. The documents showed her to be one of two aircraft making up a small charter airline. She was to load a cargo comprised of construction materials, two tons of polyester resin, and sixteen tons of fertilizer. Delivery points was to be Tunis. The customs man went over

Rafferty's papers, filled in the proper blanks and stamped them liberally.

"Routine. All in order, Sir," the man said. "We like to have your flight papers and manifest on file one hour before departure."

Rafferty thanked the man and started back to the plane. The documents were excellent forgeries. The only genuine article was the cargo contract. The manifest was dated for delivery January 4, '77. The thought of flying this particular cargo made Rafferty nervous as a cat. It frightened him more than the list of names Best had shown him in Miami, but three hundred thousand bucks quelled a lot of fear. Rafferty had meant it when he had told the man he would fly lost souls to hell for that kind of money.

He moved the old passenger plane to a hanger area where repairs had been arranged for, then checked into a hotel. In five days, he would load the cargo; in six he would retire.

***

One-ten a.m., December 28th, Joseph Grade contacted the control tower at Paris and received a course and altitude to enter the traffic pattern. Two minutes later he jabbed a switch activating a red light in the DC-3's cargo area. Ten seconds later, still twenty-three miles outside Paris, a large trunk plummeted from the rear door on the plane. Its parachute opened the seconds later three more black chutes blossomed, carrying they're passengers down through the low cloud cover.

The DC-3 landed 12 minutes later and taxied to a customs and immigration point. The plane's documents showed it had arrived from San Paulo, Brazil, via Dakar and Casablanca. The cargo was a consignment of avocados and an agriculture inspector was called.

Grade left the cargo to his Brazilian co-pilot and cleared customs. He rented a Volkswagen Van just outside the gate and drove south out of the city. It was still dark when he retrieved his three passengers and headed back into Paris. He dropped them at a railway terminal and was having breakfast before eight. After eating, he would pay Romez his prearranged fee, then spend the entire day on the town. Why not? It was Sunday in Paris and he couldn't do anything on Sunday anyway.

On the 30th he had a cargo for Brussels, so he would spend Monday collecting several items that were to be added to his cargo manifest. He would have to hire another co-pilot, but that would be simple and didn't concern him in the least. On the 4th he had a cargo out of Brussels, for Strasbourg. After delivery, like Rafferty, his intention was to retire.

***

Trains are the European way to travel. They purchased second class tickets and traveled to Brussels, via Reims. Jerry was longhaired and bearded, but well dressed. Nicole wore a blond wig and glasses. They were in appearance much like a dozen other young weekend travelers on the train as they went to meet Le Bank.

George Le Blank was an impressive man. Middle aged and in excellent physical condition, he was immaculately dressed in a style that smacked of wealth and position. In truth, George was a safe cracker. He had been contacted five days before as he walked out of prison after a six-year error in judgment. The man had just walked up and handed him an envelope with five one hundred-dollar bills, and a note requesting a little conversation. Le Blank was stupefied. He followed the man like a puppy and three hours later had agreed to take on what appeared to be the most lucrative, if not the simplest, job of his career.

Arriving in Brussels with a forged passport at 5:00 p.m. he had met his employer. He was checked into one of the better rooms of a first-class hotel, then instructed that people in general and police in particular, did not associate criminals with the better, more respectable accommodations and Le Blank wondered why the thought had never occurred to him. Dinner was sent to his room where he spent the evening doing his homework and checking out his list. "George," he told himself, "tomorrow will be a busy day."

Well before noon on Monday, Nicole had taken lease on a fourth-floor office at 12th Avenue Mass. The office was shabby and had no view, but computer blueprints of the old building showed it as one of the four offices positioned over the deposit vault of a bank on the ground floor. The Krediet Bank was an old establishment, but its vaults were bomb proof, fireproof, and virtually impregnable. The Group's computer had corroborated this, and also listed the vault as the point where its own duplicate records rested in the form of 30 cans of microfilm.

After a quick look at the office, she went downstairs and into the Krediet Bank. It took only ten minutes to rent a safety deposit box. She placed a file of blank papers in the vault several minutes later, then returned to the hotel. Tomorrow she would return and place the disk.

Jerry spent an hour after breakfast, glancing through a series of brochures and trade catalogs. They covered a wide variety of items from archery equipment to non-military pyrotechnics. He made two lists, writing the address of a manufacturer or supplier after each item. He found most of the things on his list were stocked by one prominent ship chandlery in Antwerp. He ordered by phone promising to have a banker check to them in this afternoons mail. He would require delivery by noon Tuesday.

He found the crossbow in a large sport shop in the central business district. The clerk, a short round industrious man, was only too happy to have a reel attached to the stock for fishing. Jerry also bought 150 yards of 6 lb. monofilament line, 400 ft. of 100 lb. test line, one dozen quarrels, hiking gear, night binoculars, and a camouflage hunting outfit. He paid in Francs asking that his purchases be delivered to his hotel in the morning.

Two other stops were required to secure the surveying instruments and 500 pounds of small, but powerful magnets. He had a late lunch and spent the afternoon searching for a suitable half-ton truck. He and Nicki had dinner in their room and turned in early.

***

George Le Blank rented a room in a small hotel early Monday morning, registering under the name of his forged passport and paying for two days lodging. Taking a cab directly to the airport's Pan American Cargo Terminal, he claimed and paid duty on several crates of electronic equipment, then for a small fee, arranged delivery to 12th Avenue Mass. He visited an old friend and sometime associate at his shop on Blvd., Leopold. They had worked together last on a job in Italy ten years before, but Le Blank knew him as a reliable source of materials. They had lunch together and drank afterward, speaking of successful jobs, close calls, laughing over incidents that seemed funny only in retrospect.

He was a small fat man, with bright blue eyes and a voice that demanded confidence. Le Blank had to remind himself repeatedly that the jolly little bastard couldn't be trusted as far as the door. Toward the end they talked business and a considerable number of Francs changed hands. For payment, the Belgian agreed to produce three items before 6:00 p.m. As agreed, the crates arrived at the small hotel and George Le Blank departed at 5:50 by way of the service entrance. If he had learned anything from twenty-five years in the business, it was to maintain a healthy distrust of his friends.

Tuesday morning Le Blank purchased the last of the material on his list at a large Industrial Hardware and took a cab to 12th Avenue, Mass. The girl was waiting and smiled when he let himself into the office.

"Did you put the disk in place?" he asked, closing the door behind him.

"Yes, left side of the top drawer. I slipped it into the crack between the top deposit box drawer and the edge of the vault wall," Nicole said.

"We're in business then, Ma'am," Le Blank said with a smile of his own. "Did you find out what sort of work they do in the two offices below us yet?"

"Third floor is a doctor's office, second floor an Accounting. Both of the offices are closed from 4:30 Friday afternoon until 8:00 Monday morning."

"That's nice to know Ma'am, but I don't figure on this taking me more than twelve hours once I start. He lit a cigarette, tossed his match to one side, and began to tear open his boxes of equipment. "You know, when I was a youngster, I started out in the oil business. Rough necking. Hard work, Ma'am. Was ramrod on my own rig, time I was twenty-two. Boy, I was a hell raiser back then!"

Le Blank tossed his cigarette butt into a waste basket after the match and lit another as he talked. "Decided one day that I was going to do some wildcat drilling on my own. Get rich, you know. Anyhow, me and this other old boy took drills and some Nitro and headed for this little old bank in Cameron. That's in Louisiana, next to the Texas line, ya know. We were going to blow open this bank to get our investment capital. Frank was a city boy; said we couldn't miss."

Le Blank had a Geiger counter out of its crate now and began attaching it to a dolly. "Well we busted in the back wall with a sledgehammer and crawled in. I drilled two holes in one side of the door and Frankie Capoli, he drills two behind the hinges. We pour some Nitro in the holes, then poured some more in for good measure and plug it up. You know, Ma'am, that damned vault door went clean across the street and squashed the Sheriff's dog. The whole building collapsed.

"And you and Capoli?" Nicole asked evenly.

"Beat it out of town and began to take the oil work more serious."

"And you've become a success since?" she asked.

"Well I ain't never blowed myself up and I ain't never been bored." Le Blank had the instrument mounted now, and he flipped a switch, allowing it to warm up for a moment. He began to move it slowly across the floor. "Mind moving a little bit, Ma'am and pull those there chairs out of the way please?" Nicole moved the furniture as he advanced the dolly.

Finally, Le Blank was satisfied with the pattern on the cathode ray tube. He flipped it off and marked a place beneath the instrument with red chalk. He checked the building and vault plans for a moment then measured five inches to the side and one foot back, making another red X. "There's where we drill, Ma'am. Just like going for oil in a thousand feet of water. This thing would pick up the radioactive material in that disk at a mile, he said slapping the box affectionately. Thirty-five feet down and your smack in the middle of the first box."

"That's all there is to it?"

"Yup! You run along now Ma'am. I've got a few deliveries to wait on, then I'm taking a few days off." Le Blank sat down as he spoke. "One other thing, Ma'am. I generally like to work alone. You won't need to be around Friday."

"I want to be here. It's very important that the contents of the boxes are totally destroyed," she said.

"Like the little story I told ya, Ma'am; beginners tend to mess up the works." He lit another cigarette and paused. "This is supposed to make my fortune and I don't want any little problems."

"This is my life, Monsieur. If the files exist after Saturday, I may not," she spoke softly looking straight at Le Blank from the doorway.

'Young, good looking ones always get involved with this spy shit,' he thought. So damned smart, they're stupid. Well, he wasn't; he didn't give a shit what side pulled off what; he wanted the money. To get it, he would perform his job perfectly.

"You people asked me to take on a job that the average man would have found impossible, Ma'am. Now what say you run along and let me do it."

Nicole nodded and left the office. The thing was so near to being done -- It was a nerve-racking experience that she never got used to, so she forced her mind to operate on separate levels now: one concerned with the everyday actions of living, the other with murder and masquerade. Even so, she could sense the fear and violence changing her, reaching her, distorting values. She couldn't separate herself from everything happening around her.

Jerry returned to their room late that night. She was in bed but woke at the sound of the shower. He was soaking wet when she opened the bathroom door. She handed him a towel and smiled out from behind sleepy eyes.

"You're rotten," she said.

"Yeah!"

"I was beautiful for you this evening. Now look at me," she said, pointing to her sleep ruffled hair.

He reached out and tugged the sash on her robe. As it fell open, he pulled her against him causing her to squirm and squeal.

"You're cold and wet."

"Umm, you're warm and dry," he chuckled.

They made love in the large warm bed and Nicole thought only of the moment. Later she lay curled up in the crook of his arm, feeling like a warm well-loved pet.

"Tell me something," she said, "what will we do after Saturday?"

"Go on a honeymoon and lay in the sunshine."

"No, Mon Amie. What sort of life?"

"I don't know. I really don't. I've never thought that far out," Jerry said.

"Not like now, though."

"No, not like this life," he said, hugging her to him. "We'll go someplace and be like very quiet little mice for awhile. We can decide things later."

They lay quiet for a few moments before he spoke again. "I've got everything rigged at Euro Security's building. First timer's set for 9:30 a.m. Saturday. I'm leaving for Luxembourg in the morning."

"And me?"

"Australia, only tomorrow rather than Saturday."

"You're sure?" she whispered.

"I'm sure," he said. "Watch the papers and if the men produce, you transfer the funds Monday morning.

"Oui, and what will that leave?"

Two hundred thousand that we can get our hands on safely. When all this calm down, we might become the Carlton's."

"And if it does not calm down?"

"Ha," he chuckled, "If it doesn't and you can't get by on that kind of money, I know where there's a gold mine, Nicki. Now go to sleep."

"I won't always be ordered about like this you know. I won't be ignored either."

"Sure, Honey."

"I won't."

"Yes, you will, because I'm bigger than you."

"A bigger fool," she snorted, and curled against his back. She waited a few seconds, then began nibbling the back of his shoulder.

"Oh hell," he swore, when he finally turned to embrace her.

19

TRAVEL
General
As a rule, the safest route avoids major roads and populated areas, even if it takes more time and energy. The use of natural concealment afforded by darkness, wooded areas trees, bushes, and terrain features are recommended. Remember to use all your

senses; stop, listen, smell, watch. Speed
and distance are usually of secondary importance.
FROM DEPT. OF THE ARMY FIELD MANUAL, FM 25-79

The countryside near the junction of France, Belgium, and Luxembourg was to a large degree, made up of wooded hills. Jerry drove south from Brussels toward Somnia before leaving the main road and crossed the border on a dirt track just past noon.

He left the truck outside the railway station at St. Neil's, taking the train only five miles before getting off at Marquette. He adjusted his backpack and walked away from the station toward a small food store. He entered and purchased bread, cheese, and some canned meats. After tucking it into his pack, he walked casually toward the edge of town.

It was nearly dark; the winter air was becoming crisp. He placed two smoke bombs a half mile from town and set the timers. Picking a haystack just off the road, he burrowed into its backside and slipped his pack off. He enjoyed a large slice of bread and cheese, chewing slowly and relaxing. Nicki would be in Tehran by now. With luck, he would be clear of Europe himself before Saturday and he'd read about the Bastards in Sunday's paper. They would, of course, be written up as great men of morality and integrity. Tragic deaths.

He knew what made them tick. It all boiled down to power-lust. In the world money was power; money, land, stocks, oil, were power and power had always been the name of the game. He'd known this when he was fourteen, playing the game in a small way but as seriously as any of the men he now intended to kill.

One night on the Plain of Jars, his team had been stumbled into by an enemy platoon. The unit was made up mostly of poorly trained twelve and thirteen-year olds; it was totally destroyed within 30 seconds of the first contact. Afterward they realized they could have disengaged and were disgusted at having fought children. The team leader, Les Wells had said, "If you don't want 'em dead, don't kill 'em. You can't undo death. It's final. If you're playing games to win, somebody's got to lose. If you don't like making losers, don't play." Jerry had never forgotten Well's statements.

That spring in Laos he had lost the motivation, the appetite it took to play for power. He'd outgrown it while lying in concealment, watching an enemy column pass, knowing that he could reach out and end the life of any man he saw. It gave him a new perspective. You could always do a thing, but never undo it. The choice was always yours; an act could be positive or negative, for life or for death. He wasn't a hypocrite though; they could have gone on like this forever if they hadn't affected him personally.

The one rule they broke, Jerry told himself, was don't get caught. That's the only one that counts, for no matter how important an individual is, regardless of his position, he's vulnerable. Give a man a good reason to kill you and usually he will. Well they got caught and so did I, he thought; so, did I, but they pushed the wrong guy.

It was nearly midnight when the vibrating alarm on his wristwatch woke him. He pulled on a black wool sweater, rubbed grease paint onto his face and neck, before shrugged his pack on. After checking his compass, he walked east, keeping to the woods and fields, moving in a stop-start fashion. A cool breeze blew against his face, carrying sounds of the night down to him.

A few hours before dawn he heard something ahead and spent nearly 30 minutes covering the next few hundred yards. Checking his map, he guessed himself to be within a half mile of Bon Sabreur.

It was five a.m. when he reached the stream. Upstream or down, he pondered? Up he decided. The road was round a bend and only about a hundred yards, and he nearly missed seeing two fishermen below its bridge. Backing up and circling them, he made sure he wasn't seen before advancing.

Paralleling the road, he reached the ridge line and listened for a full ten minutes before crossing. He had to climb all the way to summit before the villa came into view. Smiling at the sight he squatted and checked his compass. Seven hundred yards he figured, close enough, and he established himself in a deep crevice, bridged by a fallen oak. It was about 30 feet below the ridge line and comfortably full of leaves, but most important, it offered an excellent view of the villa. He could observe the entire southwest side of the building and some of the valley.

In the hour before dawn he made himself a light meal, and assembled his crossbow. Sunrise was beautiful in the rugged hills and Jerry promised himself to pay more attention to such things in the future. "For the moment," he told himself as he pulled out the binoculars, "staring at Bon Sabreur would have to suffice."

He had spotted the encirclement of guards before midmorning and studied them all day. He judged they amounted to a platoon sized force, 50 to 60 men, in positions at distances ranging from 400 to 500 yards from the building and he was relieved that he wouldn't have to get that far in. Most of the last 400 yards to the Villa was open lawn. They were spaced every 40 yards which sealed it off quite effectively. Research had revealed: television cameras, dogs, and guards on the road as security. If they increased the security force by this much, someone must suspect something. If so, the meeting might be shifted to another location. The thought worried him.

Late Thursday afternoon he assembled part of his equipment and put on his camouflage shirt. He waited until the shadows were long and only an hour of light remained before he left the crevice. He moved along the ridge until the buildings NW side was at 90-degree angle. It took only a few moments working with a level plate and surveyors' sextant to find the point on the hillside level with the top of Bon Sabreur walls. He slipped one of the four small black boxes from his pack placing it six feet above the ground in the bowl of a large oak, then attached an antenna wire and strung it out onto a low branch before concealing the box itself with moss. Satisfied, he circled the building repeating the process on the opposite side.

At the rear of the Villa, he removed the instruments for the third time. The building was backed against a broad shallow ravine averaging 300 yards across and rising to the ridge line from a depth of 50 feet below the walls' base. Jerry began to measure for a point bearing northwest from the center of the building and 60 feet below the top of the wall. The land fell away slowly and he found himself having to move in closer than he had expected.

Light was going fast, moreover he now had a serious problem. He was 610 yards from the wall and 50 feet below top level but 610 yards was 140 yards too close for the rear beacon.

Jerry worked a ratio problem in his head to adjust the height of the forward transmitter. The original plan called for the radios to be placed at 750 and 600 yards, with the forward box 10 feet above the rear. At 600 and 450 yards a 12-foot vertical separation would be required.

The problem rested on getting the box into the new position, a position requiring him to get over 50 yards inside their security screen. One slip and the whole damned thing would go down the drain, he thought. "You rotten bastards," he muttered under his breath, hating them for the mess he was in. He wanted an object to pass above the front wall with exactly 10 feet of clearance and for that the range was necessary. He had to place it correctly or nothing worked.

He decided that it was too dark to pick the exact spot for the forward beacon, so he would look everything over tomorrow morning, then move in and place the beacon at dark. He set the rear radio beacon, then picked out a ledge covered by thick undergrowth as his next observation point.

He was closer now, so he sprinkled powdered chlorine in a wide circle to help hide his scent. With the large number of men around the dogs wouldn't know my scent from 50 other men anyway, he figured, but I have to be careful. No chances now; put one little box in a tree and I win. He asked himself, "Was there anything more to do, anything important?" He decided not and relaxed, scooping leaves around and over himself to form a natural sleeping bag, and told himself, "Don't worry about it -- either you make it or you don't. Not easy, but not difficult. Sleep now and worry tomorrow. do it all tomorrow."

***

Thirty minutes after customs finished checking the cargo against the manifest, Rafferty began covering the stacked bags of Ammonium Nitrate fertilizer with cement and a polyester resin. He was sweating under his oxygen mask and the resin burned his skin wherever it penetrated his gloves. It took nearly two hours to seal the 300 odd bags and he grunted with satisfaction when the last case of bolts was shoveled onto the sticky heap. Smiling to himself, he guessed it would be hard as a rock by midnight.

Rafferty knelt, extracted two wires from the base of the heap, and snapped them to a second set leading to a detonator timing device at the aircraft's rear door. he paused deliberately, running through each step of the hookup in his mind. Center bag in the pile contained 100 lbs. Of Gelignite and blasting caps; wires ran to rear door activating switch; detonator would be set off by radio signal or impact of the aircraft's nose once the switch was thrown.

He flipped the ventilation switch, and turning grasped the door handle, twisted and pushed. Pulling the oxygen mask down he took a deep breath of fresh air, and enjoyed the luxury of a broad grin. Everything was set up the way James Best had instructed. One short flight and Doug Rafferty was going to be what his ex-wife never expected when she left him -- A rich man.

***

At three o'clock Friday afternoon, Etienne Prost accepted a check written on the Societe General de Banque. He got the aircraft's young pilot's receipt for the twenty, 55-gallon drums of Acetone and headed for the center of Brussels with the boxes Grade had given him for delivery. His last delivery was made to the offices of Euro Security at 4:15 p.m. the six rolls of computer paper, and the boxes of peripheral supplies were placed in the freight elevator at the rear of the building.

One of the janitors signed his receipt and wished him an enjoyable weekend. Etienne checked his watch and decided that if he was to be in time for his son's birthday part, he had better hurry. The janitor put the consignment of computer supplies in a fourth-floor supply area adjacent to the computer room. It was a Friday afternoon and the clerk had left a few minutes early as was the custom on Fridays. The janitor put the receipts on his desk and went downstairs to punch the time clock. It was 4:45 p.m.

***

At the airport, Joe Grade had just completed securing the drums of acetone. He cleared his cargo with customs and filed his papers for a 7:00 a.m. take-off destination, Strasbourg, Germany. He called his co-pilot several minutes later to tell him the flight was off. Sorry! He would see him on Monday.

Joe was going to fly this one himself, but not to Strasbourg. He made a careful check of his equipment and returned to his hotel. It would be a damned long night, he thought.

A half hour after the end of the business day, George Le Blank drilled his first hole. It was precisely 5 inches in diameter. He lowered a fourteen-foot section of rigid plastic pipe into the hole until it stopped on the floor below. It took an additional 30 minutes to align the pipe and set up to drill through it.   The four-and-a-half-inch diameter bit punched through the ceiling plaster of the second-floor accountant office at 6:05 p.m.   Le Blank added two more sections of shaft to the drill extending the bit to the floor; he aligned and cut through the thick oak floor, then retrieved his bit and drill shaft.   He lowered a steel pipe with a bearing at each end and a 4 ½ inch outside diameter into the first pipe.   It slid through the ceiling of the accountant's office, down eleven feet, slipping neatly into the hole in the floor.

There would be three feet of reinforced concrete below it, then three inches of steel.   Le Blank attached a water-cooling line leading down into the hole and began to set up the heavy-duty drilling gear.   Doug Kershaw sang "Diggy, Diggy Lo" from a small cassette, Le Blank had purchased the day before.   He hummed along with the Cajun music, puffing vigorously on his cigarette.   "Great to be back at work George," he told himself, while attaching a one-inch drill bit.

20

TRAVEL
General
Whenever possible, the terrain to be traveled
during the night should be observed during
the daylight hours. Be particularly attentive
to the concealment. It will provide, the enemy
or natural obstacles over or around which you
are to travel.

FROM: FR 25-79

Stretched under the lip of the ridge Jerry looked down, concentrating on the area he would pass through. He had studied the ground all day mentally mapping his route to a large oak at the ravine's bottom. At a few minutes past seven, he began crawling down the hill.

He reached the position of the first beacon easily and attached the end of a 450-foot length of monofilament line to a sapling. Checking his bearings once more, he began to edge down slope again, staying low, using every bit of cover. After what he guessed to be ninety yards, he spotted one of them and stopped.

He was abreast the man and would be placing the transmitter within 80 yards of him. There would be others too, maybe closer, and the underbrush had been cleared on the lower slope. He slowly scooped leaves against his side, waiting for the night to grow darker. After a few moments the combination of excitement and immobility caused an almost irresistible urge to squirm, move, do something, anything just to break the tension building in him.

'Control yourself, you dumb twit,' he thought. Hell, what is there to worry about? This is a camping trip; you would have been laughed out of Special Forces school for getting worked up like this. Relax, relax, and calm yourself. Think of what you're going to do again.

Jerry's thoughts began to move outward; he began to relax as he casually watched the man on his left, studied the clump of shrub thirty yards to his right where he knew another man lay hidden. Then slowly almost imperceptibly, he began working his way down into the ravine. When the monofilament line ran out, he looked up.

High and slightly off to the side he could make out the dead limb he had picked that morning. The box must be at that exact level. The tree had no lower branches, but he had considered that problem earlier. He passed a fine tough thread from the reel mounted on the crossbow, through a ring at the end of a specially fitted quarrel, clipping it back to the stock. He aimed carefully, squeezed and the short arrow thunked into the tree. He attached the radio beacon to the cord and pulled it up into the tree until it jammed against the arrow, clipping itself in place. The line fell clear and he reeled it in before reloading the crossbow.

So, intent was he in what he was doing that the violent jerk on the monofilament line took him completely by surprise. He was already rolling onto his back, hearing someone cursing under his breath; then he was looking at the man's shape 30 feet behind him, swinging the crossbow around until suddenly a quarrel was protruding from the man's throat, rather than resting atop the bow. Jerry glanced to the side again; a shape was moving cautiously out of the shrub to his right, hesitating, trying to ascertain what the rapid sequence of motion had been.

Jerry worked the crank feverishly, re-cocking, placing another quarrel on the crossbow. The man called something low in Flemish, which Jerry couldn't quite catch. No! No! You bastard, he thought; don't give me away you loud mouth son-of-a-bitch. He a was peering intently, twenty yards now, and his sub-machine gun began to swing toward Jerry. There was a faint hum; the man pitched over clawing at a wooden stub in his chest, fighting for the breath to scream, his gun rattling against the rocks.

'No noise; God no noise.' Jerry was already scrambling toward him, pulling his knife, clutching with his left hand, driving in hard with the right, jerking the blade up from the stomach, into the chest cavity.

"Raoul?" a voice questioned.

Jerry spun. The man was too close to hide from. He saw him a split second too late, raced toward him, the gun was coming up, he was reaching, thrusting with the knife, wrenching the muzzle aside. The man twisted, kicked expertly catching him in the hip knocking him back off balance. The gun clattered on the rocks; the guard leaped for it. Jerry scrambled back toward him but the guard managed to reach the gun, fingering the trigger, aiming as Jerry's knife flashed. The heat, light of muzzle blast blinded him, threw him jerking, spinning back to land on one side stunned, rolling face down. His hand against his left side was warm, sticky. It didn't hurt; it was numb, paralyzed. Oh god, what now? I'm hit. Got to move, get away.

He squirmed, managed to stand, then staggered up-hill tripping over the guard, falling again. You did it, didn't you, you bastard. You fixed me good. He pulled his shirt open as he staggered up again, feeling for his wound. There were two holes, in and out where it had passed through, near the surface. He picked up the machine pistol and holding his side, he labored up the hill. He felt a tug at his belt. The damned monofilament line, he thought, have to bring it. Stupid luck, him tripping over the line; worse luck for you than me buddy.

Voices were yelling to each other all around him now. The woods were filled with the sound of snapping branches, men running; he could hear dogs barking in the distance. The line was stuffed in his pocket and he raced cross slope, hand tight against his side, stumbling in pain, the wound slowing in spite of himself.

'Run now; rest later; think later,' his fear urged. 'No. Think now! Think on your feet,' he told himself. 'What can I do? Dogs. I can't outrun dogs now, I'm hurt. Damit, there's always something to do, always a way! Always! Think, you shit; they're going to kill you if you don't think!'

***

Three dead, no more than two minutes ago, and nobody's seen him yet. "Jesus, God," Van Riebeeck shouted, charging back into the gatehouse, the door smashing behind him.

"Get the dogs out there! Get the helicopter!" He was rushing across the room to the radio, excited that the man was in his trap, irritated at the same time. The door slammed behind the pilot, running for the shed that covered his machine. Van Riebeeck slapped at the radio's switches, yelled into the microphone. "Morroit! Morroit! Come in damned you. Morroit!"

There was no answer, then, "Benois here, Sir."

"Get Morroit you idiot!" the Dutchman cursed.

"He's organizing things outside, Sir," Benois answered.

Don't act impulsively, Van Riebeeck made himself, calm down. He could hear yelping outside the wall, then a chorus of howls as the dogs picked up the scent and gave voice. He was on the phone now, excitement easing; he was reminding himself less of a foolish woman, and more of himself. "Inspector Palus, Karl Van Riebeeck here." He spoke rapidly, giving an impression of outrage while reporting the murder of three employees at Bon Sabreur. He gave a good description of Carlton to the police official and was insured that prompt discreet action would be taken.

"So much for legality," Van Riebeeck muttered hanging up, and strode outside where the high whine and flapping sound of the helicopter was drowning out the other noise. He weighed the value of the machine and decided against operating from it. Instead, he sent Harold Desorm and moved off at a trot to where the dogs were barking.

It took only moments to discover the man had been wounded. His first order was to turn the Dobermans loose. Four good tracking hounds were kept on leash and he and his men pressed through the dark after them. Chances were excellent that the Dobermans would bring Carlton down, leaving only dead meat to capture; at the very least they should affect to slow him down. As he became surer of direction, he radioed the information to enable interception.

The men Van Riebeeck ran with were young and he struggled to match their pace. He was breathing so fast and deep that his lungs were burning, but he knew how to run and kept a smooth regular stride waiting for his second wind to come. As a young man he could run tirelessly. He had been born in Semarang, on the Island of Java, and educated in Europe during the late thirties. He had fought the Germans as an officer of the Dutch Royal Army during the Second World War. With the rapid defeat of the Netherlands, he had escaped to England fighting and rising to Major at the age of twenty-four. The late forties found him fighting on his home ground, the Dutch East Indies, against insurgent Indonesian forces.

It was a military experience that suited his natural talents. He was rapidly promoted to full Colonel and guerrillas in areas under his command, were promptly irradiated. The subtleties of his methods were matched only in their ruthlessness; otherwise he was considered a conservative, scrupulously able, and patriotic man of integrity.

In 1949 two incidents joined to alter Van Riebeek's outlooks, his sense of values. One was of major historical importance; one was very minor when viewed on a world scale, for when a fanatic Moslem terrorist broke into the Van Riebeeck home in Semarang, hacking his wife and children to death with a machete, the war had progressed in the favor of the Dutch. It was all but won. Then orders came to pull out, turning the country over to Nationalists under Sukano and Hatta. Against order, Van Riebeeck personally hunted and killed the terrorists. He put the man on public display in Semarang, then hacked him to death before a crowd in the central plaza. He resigned his commission in disgust and fled the country to survive. His fortune was in land and in the end, Karl Van Riebeeck lost all.

For eleven years he drifted, earning a living wherever top money was paid for military expertise. He became known in elite circles as an organizer of rare ability and the sixties found him in Katanga when Toushombe seceded from the Congo. His activities, undertaken on contract in behalf of certain mining interests were as successful as they were brilliant. They lead to his present position and the forming of Euro Secur. The group were his patrons; the organization was his creation. It performed its function smoothly in a world where almost nothing performed smoothly, that is until this man altered the situation. He'd see the man dead.

The dogs were barking, coughing; the handlers legs pumping, feet scrambling ahead. Van Riebeeck, straining to keep up, wondered for the thousandth time why his organization had been unable to cope with Carlton. Then it came to him. For the same reason Euro Secur would not be effective against himself; Carlton for all effects, was a man extremely similar to himself, Van Riebeeck thought. He is much as I was years ago. I am hunting myself, my alter ego.

It was a rare privilege to face such a challenge. He almost hoped Carlton would escape the Dobermans, extending the hunt, he almost loved the man, but he feared him more; he would kill him none the less. Van Riebeek's legs were being drained of energy now. They cleared the ridge and quickened the pace.

208

He yelled to the dog handler, "Slow down damit, we wish to kill him, not ourselves."

21

SURVIVAL EVASION AND ESCAPE
6-3 Evasion Techniques
When evading alone avoid panic, overcome
fear and shock and think before acting.
Recall any previous briefing, SOP, or
training and choose a course of action.
Assess those factors to your advantage;
terrain, cover, weather, water, weapons,
etc.; also considering those to your
advantage before selecting a course of action
Maintain self-control and think the problem through.
- FROM ARMY FIELD
MANUAL 25-79

Jerry zigzagging downhill hit the stream at a run. He had judged it to be close but had not seen it until he was falling into it. Scrambling to his feet, he waded to the far bank nearly losing his footing on stones and submerged logs. A half-mile, he thought, lurching into the bank and starting to run again. He felt better, was glad he had fallen into the water; it gave him a sense of energy, of wellbeing.

The sound of the dogs changed. Baying was wild now coming at him. How to throw off the scent. How to fool the dogs. Think! Think! The road, run to the road, then backtrack and jump in the stream. They might think you were picked up by a car. It might confuse them, buy time. How far he asked himself, trying to visualize the area from memory. A hundred yards no more. The pain was searing, he couldn't let it hold him back; you can stop and rest if you make it, or rest forever if you don't.

It was so dark under the trees that he ran head long into a man who was running in the opposite direction without seeing him. He heard the crack of his head smacking into the other man, his breath exploded before he ever saw him. They rebounded from each other falling hard, dazed. Jerry rolled; he fought for breath rising on hands and knees, crawling toward the man. Swinging wide, weakly, he cracked the man upside of his head with the machine pistol, driving him to the ground.

Jerry was becoming dizzy. Too much blood he told himself. Have to stop the flow. Later, later. First get clear of the dogs, no time for the road now, can't make the road. You have to make the road though. No, you don't. Mix the scent; confuse them.

Frantically, he wiped blood from his wounds on the man, on his pants, shoes. He shook him, slapped him conscious, pulled him to his feet. "Run," he yelled in French. "Run or I shoot." The man staggered, took a few steps stumbling then regaining his senses, he bolted into the dark the way he had come. Taking the man's weapon as well as his own, Jerry dashed back toward the stream, lungs aching, heart pounding. He saw it ahead now; he could hear the dogs close, bushes crashing; he dove, feeling the cold water over him, letting the current carry him.

How long can you hold your breath? Two minutes, three? No. More like one minute. He heard splashing nearby, dogs crossing the stream then silence. He counted his heart beats, twenty, forty; go to a hundred, he ordered himself. His head broke the surface at sixty-five, his chest expanding with the pure ecstasy as the oxygen rushed into his lungs. He gulped the air, pulled in huge rasping gasps of it, his eyes darting side to side. Suddenly he could hear growls in the distance, screams, mindless screams. Ha! Enjoy yourself, he thought. Do a good job on him so they won't figure it out for a while.

He heard baying coming from his left now too; it was getting louder, closer. Two groups, he thought. NO! They let one pack of dogs loose and are trailing with the other. He staggered downstream, held his breath where the stream passed under the bridge, guns weighing him down, current carrying him past.

Five minutes later he pulled himself onto an island midstream, a rock with a few trees really. He was dizzy and could hardly breath now; the refreshing effects of the cold water had become debilitating. His clothes were clinging to him, icy wet, and he fought to control his shivering. His side ached, rather than burned. He would have to fix it now, right now.

He pulled his sweater off, then his undershirt. He scrapped moss from the trees, then bound it against the wounds with the folded undershirt, securing it with his belt. Pulling the wool sweater back on, he lay back, scraping leaves and pine needles around himself for warmth. He stuffed them in his shirt and pants for insulation and lay resting. One hour he told himself; one hour to get your strength, then move. He could hear shouts and gunfire in the distance, and the sound made him feel good. Let them mill around while he rested. This was his kind of fight; he had been trained for it, and even wounded he could beat them. Hell, he'd beaten them now; even if Van Riebeeck killed him, he'd beaten them.

He tried to form a picture of Van Riebeeck from memory; tall, tanned, rugged looking, standing on the roadside, pursuing him along the bank of the African river; Karl Van Riebeeck, hand of the enemy. I'll kill him before this is over Jerry promised himself; I'll kill him, but not now. I've got to rest now, just rest.

***

The truck backed up to the roadside, and four men tossed the body into the back. They had had one hell of a time getting the Dobermans off the body. The face and throat had been torn to shreds confusing the issue of several minutes, but a quick check of the body showed no gunshot wounds. A closer inspection pointed to an older man than Carlton.

"Paaft! More than one," Van Riebeeck swore. He stood at the side of the dark road, shook his head and walked slowly around the truck. "Any word?" he asked a man inside with the radio.

The man outlined against the headlights, nodded the affirmative. "Two of our people wounded a few minutes ago; they shot each other."

"Fools," he said. Well he had to be somewhere near. Wounded and on foot he would not make it. The dogs would pick up his scent again, and he would be caught. No Dobermans this time though. Let the hounds find him.

The handler had managed to calm the hounds, and as the truck pulled away he began to work them. There were four of them, noses to the ground, excited, barking, withers trembling. The man moved them side to side, along the road and in a hundred-foot radius of where the Dobermans had killed. Nervous, the dogs jerked their heads around at far off sounds, their nostrils quivering. Each time the handler worked them they pulled off in the direction they had approached from.

The man scratched his head, looking regretfully at Van Riebeeck. "Either he escaped by car of they are confused as to what scent to follow," he said. "Do you have something with his smell?"

"Yes," Van Riebeeck said, "Ernst, the radio."

A man rose from a log at the roadside hurrying, fumbling with a small portable radio.

"Call and have the knapsack sent here immediately," he ordered, "and Ernst, tell them to rub it in some of the blood leading up from the ravine." Van Riebeeck walked to a large rock and sat. He reached for his pipe from habit; disgruntled when he realized he had not brought it, he checked his watch. Eight twenty. He needed time to ready himself for questions at tomorrow's meeting and this was taking much too much time. Impatience would add nothing to the effort; better to think on his terms for the moment. What would I have done faced with his problem? Van Riebeeck asked himself.

He visualized him, running, dogs behind him, limping; the other man pulling ahead, then the river. That's it he thought, I would have stayed in the river; I would have let the animals take my accomplices trial, used the diversion to escape in another direction. Van Riebeeck could see him wading in the stream, covering distance, picking a safe spot to rest and attend his wounds.

When the knapsack arrived fifteen minutes later, they moved the dogs back toward the river. Sixty meters from the road the dogs became excited, pulling forward and Van Riebeeck noticed something he had missed as they hurried in the other direction earlier, an area filled with scruff marks, disturbed leaves. At the edge he found bloodstains and a pair of broken glasses.

What is this, he wondered, squatting and wiping his hair back? Seconds later the radio crackled and a scratchy voice advised him that the body was that of one, Andre Moise, one of Marriot's group. "My God," Van Riebeeck swore. He had taken the man here, mixed the scent and back tracked. He had used Moise as live bait, to buy time. Well, he would have no more time. He checked his watch again. Nearly 8:30 p.m.

***

The concrete had caused more trouble than Le Blank anticipated. He had ruined three bits on steel reinforcing rods and nearly burned up a fourth, but the three inches of steel was easier. When the drill punched through he continued, deeper until he penetrated a thin layer of steel below.

With satisfaction, he began lifting and dismantling the drill shaft. Halfway through the task, he stopped and reached for another cigarette, discovering he was out. "Shee-it," he swore, and went back to work. When the last section of drill shaft and the bit came clear of the hole, he crossed the room picking up the last lengths of pipe. They were one inch in diameter rigid plastic. Fitting together he lowered them into the shaft, twisting and working them until the end slipped through into the vault.

There was an audible click and the music stopped as the tape ran out on his cassette. He took the time to put in another tape and as the music played, he reviewed the job for a moment, making sure he had forgotten nothing before continuing. It was all done exactly as planned, he decided and walking to a crate near the door, he pried the lid off, removing several small containers. His hands moved swiftly as he removed the lids, placed a funnel in the pipe and began pouring in the magnesium pellets. From time to time he wiggled the pipe slightly lifting it to help the flow.

With the last of the magnesium clear of the pipe Le Blank twisted two electrical wires together and slid them into the pipe. Satisfied he stood and stretched, put on his coat and picked up the cassette recorder. Opening the door, he checked the hall. Good. Empty, he thought.

Le Blank led the wire from the shaft to the wall, paused for a split second, and with a broad grin shoved the plug into the wall socket. Smoke was rising from the shaft before he cleared the door, and as he walked down the hall toward the rear stairwell, he pictured the white-hot magnesium burning its way down through the safety deposit box, the microfilm files melting under intense heat before the burning metal actually reached them.

A strange job, George, he told himself, but done with a certain amount of class. He was out of the building walking south when the first fire alarm went off at eight forty-five.

22

Evasion

8-4

To avoid being killed or captured by enemy forces searching the battle area, leave the immediate area of action as soon as possible, and select a hiding place at a safe distance. Prepare a plan of action before leaving the hiding place.

The time you remain in this initial location is governed by hostile activity, your physical condition, and patience. This "hole-up-time" should be used to regain strength, and to evaluate the evasion problem. When you choose to move, use a prepared plan. Alternate plans of action must be developed to cope with as many eventualities as possible.

FROM ARMY FM 25-79

Jerry woke; he was frightened for a second; he didn't know how long he had dozed.   His stupor cleared and he checked his watch, only forty minutes; he sighed with relief. It was quiet. Bright stars and a full moon filled the sky. The night had become very cold; he could feel it on his face and hands, and a slight breeze was rustling branches above. He moved, propping himself on an elbow and sent pain pulsing through his side; cold air against his back caused him to shiver convulsively.   Somehow upstream he could hear a motor starting up, and the occasional yelping of dogs. There was another faint sound beyond that, the sound of a helicopter. He would have to be well clear by daylight he knew, for he couldn't handle the helicopter with everything else.

Daylight hell, he told himself; they're going to have my ass cold in two hours if I don't get moving. Which way though, which way?   He regarded the possibilities of getting back into the water and moving down stream but dismissed the idea. Even if he could stand the prolonged cold, they would be sure to have it covered. They would be confused for the moment, yes, but Van Riebeeck would be using the time to reorganize. He would figure out what had happened and start tracking along the river soon if he hadn't already.

Jerry meditated for a moment. No. The dogs weren't making the right kind of noise; they weren't tracking yet; it might work. If I really push it might work. They'll expect me to move away from them, so I'll move toward them instead. He imagined himself wading ashore and running back toward the bridge, crossing the road, then wading back into the stream. He would leave the stream where he first entered it running away from Bon Sabreur, only this time he would head back towards the Villa. Right past it and out the other side where they wouldn't expect him.

They would cover the riverbank and find a trail entering the water, only they would assume the trail was coming out of the water and they would be backtracking him without knowing it. What a joke on the sons-of-bitches. Even if he had died he would have had the last laugh, but rising to his feet, he suddenly knew it wasn't going to be that easy. He trembled and swayed on rubber legs and had to put out a hand to steady himself against a tree. He was so weak all of a sudden, he didn't know for sure if he could walk five yards, let alone run five hundred. Hell, you have to do it and if you aren't sure, you might as well find out trying.

Hanging both guns over his right shoulder he waddled into the stream. It was shallow, hip deep, but swift moving and he had trouble maintaining his balance. The effort exhausted him and dropping to his hands and knees on shore, he was sick. He felt hot and cold flashes and tried to remember his training. Replace fluids, he thought, and crawling back to the stream he drank several handfuls of water.

Pulling the magazine from one of the machine-guns, he emptied it shoving the bullets into his pockets. He replaced the magazine, then tossed the weapon onto the bank and began to walk. After a minute he forced himself to run, each stride causing a pain to jab through his left side but gritting his teeth he continued to push himself. His direction began to wobble and he ran against a tree striking his shoulder, rebounded and rolled several feet.

He lay stunned for a moment gasping, then forced himself back on his feet. You can rest later – at the road; you can rest for a minute and if you beat them to that spot in the stream, you can relax for twenty minutes. I'll give you twenty minutes. When he reached the road, his knees buckled and he dropped between two large trees. He lay sprawled there, breathing deeply, blinking perspiration out of his eyes. One hundred eighty feet away was the bridge, but there was no one on it. No one he could see. "Have to take the chance," he whispered, then thought, 'Jesus, I said that out loud.'

He was starting to rise, when he heard the car coming. He fell face down on the damp grass motionless until it passed, then sprung and ran across behind it, hoping the headlights would blind anyone looking from the direction of the bridge. He held himself motionless on the far side of the road and stared after the car. It slowed, pulling to a stop a hundred yards past the bridge.

Jerry was frightened for a moment, then he spotted the dogs in the car's headlights. He saw the driver climbing from the car, handing the bag to someone by the roadside; not a bag, his knapsack. Seconds later the dogs were yelping, barking excitedly and Jerry was up and running. Brambles caught him full in the face tearing at him as he plunged through a thicket. Twenty yards ahead he saw the stream again and staggering to a stop, he turned and backed across the soft muddy ground and into the water.

Close now, a few minutes now. That was all. His left hand pressed against his side now as he stumbled along in the knee-deep water. He fell without having tripped. Jesus, I haven't done that before. He fell again wetting his face and rising to his feet realized he was at the place, the location where he had originally entered the stream.

It was steep, and he leaned into the hill digging with his feet, keeping to the ground that was torn up with tracks. He could hear the dogs coming right at him, and he scrambled faster, went to crawling, dragging the machine gun, desperate to reach the top, waiting for a light to strike him, to expose him. The land leveled out abruptly and Jerry collapsed, wriggling over the spine of the ridge, breathing in ragged breaths, giggling in near hysteria, crying at the same time. Control yourself. You've got it made now, so watch them, don't screw up now, not after all this.

Turning, Jerry faced downhill, watching as a number of dark shapes burst out of the trees below him. There was a loud splash and swearing as the dogs pulled their handler into the stream after them. They lunged against the leashes pulling the man across the stream on his stomach, trying to charge up the slope toward Jerry. There was a moment's confusion as other men ran forward grabbing the master leash, dogs still straining up the ridge. Jerry swung the sub-machinegun down slope and waited, hardly breathing.

He could see them clearly in the moonlight, all milling around, dogs jerking, tangling the men in the leashes. The handler was up, unsnapping individual animals from the master leash, passing them to others. Jerry's eyes went to a tall man, standing calmly off to the side. He knew him, had seen him before. His heart was pounding and his head ached horribly; waves of nausea and dizziness swept him. He wondered if he was dying, for if he was he wanted to kill Karl Van Riebeeck first.

The barrel of machine pistols lined up with Van Riebeek's chest while the question of death absorbed most of Jerry's thinking. He wanted to pull the trigger, but it would be a mistake if he was going to survive. God, how he wanted to kill him; not only because of Africa, but now for being hurt and hunted and terrified. Jerry had never been terrified, not while he was awake and facing things. In Africa he hadn't been terrified; he had been stunned, consumed with anger, but not afraid. No, that was wrong. He had been in terror when the jeep went into the river with Connie. When he knew she was dead, he hadn't been afraid anymore. That was it. You had to have something to lose in order to fear. Blinking his eyes clear, he sighted on the big man below; he thought of Nicole, pictured her, remembered her and knew why they frightened him.

The longer he lay contemplating the better he felt, warm, luxuriant, relaxed. Too much to live for, to die anymore. That's why he had been afraid. He rested his forehead on the machine gun for an instant; he was tired but he wasn't going to die. When he looked up again they were gone. That startled him for a moment until the gradual realization sunk in; he had passed out. How long, he wondered and looked at his watch. Jesus! One fifteen, over two hours.

***

The sound of water rushing made it difficult to hear the now weak radio. A man listened, though marking the positions as they came over the radio while someone held a flashlight for him. When he finished, the map was passed to Van Riebeeck who sat on a log and studied it. Van Riebeeck was cold, wet, tired, and worse he was beaten. He accepted the idea easily, being more irritated than apprehensive. After a hot trail in the beginning and finding where Carlton had entered the river and holed up, they had lost him completely.

Possibly he had drowned. The river had been covered at three points below the bridge and he would have been seen. There was no question about it. His men were good enough not to have let Carlton pass, even in the dark. He may have swum past one but the water was cold and no one could have stayed in it for four miles.

He should have turned back, but he didn't. Instead, he had hurried along covering both banks of the stream, scrambling over rocks, slipping in mud until thirty minutes became an hour, and the hour became two, and then three and he knew he was wasting his time. He had lost the man. He had spent months of long hard work to get close to him and now he had lost. Well it was over. He had his chance and lost the contest. His only emotion was empty disgust and God knows what Carlton would try next. Van Riebeeck faced the fact that this sort of security could not be maintained indefinitely. Perhaps the man had even succeeded at what he had come here for.

Was he detected on his way in or out; could he have placed a bomb? Paaft! The possibilities were limitless. Perhaps, the time had come to take his leave for, if indeed, Carlton did manage to liquidate a number of the group, they would be much less concerned with searching for the corpse of an ex-security director. Yes, Van Riebeeck decided positively, I will suffer a fatal accident, and retire to Argentina. He would find good reason to be in a small plane over open water during the day, but when the aircraft crashed, he would be elsewhere.

So, decided, he radioed instructions for the helicopter to pick him up immediately. There would be much to do before the morning's meeting, particularly since he was not expecting to attend. Of course, Marriot was advised to continue the search just in case. The possibility for blind luck always existed and should be taken into account. After all, Van Riebeeck told himself, one never knew.

23

SURVIVAL14-3
Will to survive. The determination to survive must be
maintained at times by sheer will power,
and it should be recognized that many
obstacles to be overcome are mental
rather than physical.
Hunger, thirst, pain, and other normally
Insufferable conditions must be accepted
as normal and must be endured. A strong
will to survive, together with an ability to
withstand hardships are mandatory.
FROM: ARMY FM 25-79

The moon was lower now, casting weak shadows on the ground and Jerry walked north perpendicular to the shadows, keeping the moon to his left. He had to think out each step at first, until he lapsed into a mechanical rhythm. No hurry now. Just cover ground and conserve your strength; make believe your body belongs to someone else; keep your mind sharp. Think of good things like food, and Nicki, think about Nicki.

He could hear the drone of a helicopter approaching from behind and stopped, instinctively leaning against a tree, but the machine landed somewhere and the night became silent again. He listened for noises in the woods, but didn't hear any; he began moving again, one foot after the other.

About four fever and chills began to flash through his body. Heat and then cold, heat and cold, over and over the sequence repeated itself. Warmth and food is what I need he told himself; warmth and food, but I'll have them later; one more mile first. He was growing weak fast again, so fast that he was afraid he would fall and might not be able to get up again. He had turned west at two a.m. and was in open pastureland now. Ahead he could make out a road.

He had picked his way along a fence, nervous at being in the open, so exposed. He reached a ditch and knelt, cupping the water, drinking slowly, wetting his face, his neck. For a moment the water revived him, and he continued toward the road, but crossing the plowed field was really bad. He kept stumbling in the furrows, staggering off to the side. Finally, he tripped falling hard, sending pain pulsing through his body. 'Van Riebeeck, you pig, it's your pain. I don't hurt, you do,' he told himself, struggling back to his feet. 'Nothing like you're going to hurt though. You're going to die, not me! You,' Jerry promised.

He managed to cross a fence line but eighty feet from the road he could go no further. There was a haystack a short distance to his left and he managed to reach it, slumping down in the sweet-smelling straw. Something crumpled under his hand, a wrapper, the indentation in the stack was directly in front of him. He half laughed at himself. Of all the places to end up. A half-mile from Marquette in the damned haystack, two hundred feet from the smoke bomb and eighty off the road to Bon Sabreur. It was quite a joke, but he was too sick to laugh.

If he was still alive tomorrow, he could watch the whole thing. Anger flashed in him for an instant. If – Shit! He was going to be alive. All he needed was warmth and rest, a chance to beat the fever, to regain his energy. He wouldn't move again, until he was stronger. "Five-fifteen," he whispered. I'll sleep until ten, move on at noon, be a lot of excitement by then, nobody will pay attention. Steal a car and drive into France, thirty miles, only thirty miles, and by then nobody will care to chase me.

***

The message arrived at Baptist's apartment at seven thirty Saturday morning. He went immediately to the Krediet Banque, where an officer escorted him and four other Euro Secur executives into the safety deposit vault. A Captain of the fire department explained what had destroyed the boxes and the bank officer asked discreetly what they had contained. Baptiste answered truthfully, duplicate records on microfilm. There was a short period of discussion, and questions asked by the police that led nowhere before they left.

They arrived at Euro Secur's offices at nine twenty-five and put a call through to Van Riebeeck in Luxembourg. He took the news very calmly, in Adrian's opinion, then ordered that the records be duplicated as soon as possible. The call had just ended when acrid black smoke began pouring out of the air-conditioning vents. Seconds later the fire alarm went off, however, people had already begun to evacuate the building.

Baptiste was on the ground floor before the possibility of a diversion occurred to him. Locating three security guards he charged back up to the third floor arriving just as the fuel oil tanks exploded in the basement. Fire and black smoke burst out of the ground floor windows; the sound of sirens began to penetrate the building.

"Quick, the fire escape," one of the security men yelled, running through the door of the fourth-floor supply room. Baptiste managed to take two steps in the same direction before a series of powerful explosions destroyed the entire fourth floor.

The time bombs, each five pounds of gelignite, each surrounded by 50 lbs. of small but powerful magnets, detonated within a second of each other. The computer room was demolished and little that was identifiable remained of the four men. When experts were brought in later to salvage what was possible of the computer tapes, it was found that the magnets had been blown like shrapnel in all directions, embedding themselves in walls and machinery. They had effectively erased every piece of the magnetic tape. On the basis of intelligence, Euro Secur ceased to exist as did the records of a titanic multi-national syndicate, at 0930 a.m.

***

At nine thirty-five Rafferty leaned over to look out the cockpit window. Far below sunlight painted a winding river with gold. Studying the landscape from five thousand feet, he ignored any aspects of beauty, concentrating on picking up his landmarks. From the river his eyes traveled to a large city, then south along a railroad to a small village and the village gave him the proper orientation. He flipped a switch, starting a steady beeping signal in the cockpit. Rafferty smiled slightly, but his hands shook as he throttled back slightly and began to bank the Constellation to come onto an easterly course.

Fifteen miles, he thought, and checked his watch, nine forty. Ahead, almost imperceptible beyond the village, he saw smoke. Rafferty moved quickly now, flipping switches, unbuckling his seat belt. The beep, beep, became a monotone as the big aircraft lined up on the range and he switched the controls over to the Auto pilot which locked in on the range. He could feel the plane beginning to descend slightly, gaining speed as it sought to align itself with the vertical range; he hurried toward the rear door.

Rafferty felt panicked as if he couldn't move fast enough. Reaching the door, he knelt, pressing the switch with trembling hands. An urgent alarm began to ring, signaling the arming of the explosives. Sweat pouring out of him now, Rafferty stood; a recorded 'mayday' was being transmitted now, the frantic report of a midair collision going out on distress frequencies.

Shifting under the straps of his parachute webbing, he took off a strap, then pressed the emergency release on the door. There was a small explosion as the door blew into space and a hurricane whipped into the aircraft. Squinting through the door, he felt the plane leveling off, slowing speed, the marker ahead, village flashing below, and he jumped. The parachute seemed to take forever to open, then he was floating down, spinning, swinging on the straps, watching the plane grow smaller in the distance, black smoke pouring out behind.

The DC3 passing three hundred feet above him, frightened him so badly that he lost control of himself. He hadn't been able to see it due to the canopy above, and it sounded as if it was coming straight at him. He twisted his head looking back to the west and there he was, Joe Grade beneath another white parachute drifting down out of the sky. Damn, I actually did it, he thought.

***

The phone call from Baptiste not only made up his mind, it gave Van Riebeeck the plausible excuse he needed to leave abruptly. The meeting had begun at nine. Minutes had been read and pertinent current events were still being covered when the call came for him. He left immediately, walking quickly from the main hall, across the courtyard and out past the gatehouse. He dismissed his driver and wheeled the Mercedes out through the packed parking area. Within moments, he was moving west toward Marquette at over a hundred and thirty kilometers per hour.

He was seven kilometers west of Bon Sabreur when the aircraft passed low overhead, trailing smoke. Thirty seconds later a second passed, startling him, as he had been looking back over his shoulder at the first. Ahead the country road was covered with smoke, and he had to slow down, diverting his full attention back to driving.

The old Constellation crossed the ridge at 260 MPH, eighty feet above the ground. Some of the chauffeurs and guards had heard the approaching engines, but the aircraft's glide path was so low that they were unable to see it until it cleared the ridge. Some tried to run, others took cover behind cars. The nose cleared the outer wall by ten feet and plied into the main building erupting in an explosion so violent, that it flattened the walls. It sheared trees off flat for a radius of over two hundred yards, and tossed limousines end over end across the parking area.

With the trees, went the range and the DC3 dipped low, barely clearing the ridge and bellying into the parking area. It skipped once, nosed in, and exploded carrying a white-hot ball of flaming liquid chemicals into the crater that had been a building second before.

Van Riebeeck was nearly clear of the smoke when he heard the boom. The shock wave pushed against the rear of the car seconds later as he slammed on the brakes, pulling to the side of the road. The second explosion jarred him as he was climbing from the car. The noise was deafening even at that distance and his hands went to his ears.

"He has done it," Van Riebeeck said out loud. "And I knew, I knew," he thought as he scrambled off the road into the field. The smoke was drifting down the road and he didn't have to run far into the field to see the gigantic ball of fire and smoke rising into the clear blue sky. He walked slowly, shocked, staring at debris still plummeting down from the sky.

"Mein Gott," he thought, "the worldwide repercussions of this -- the power struggles -- the changes in history." The operations and events already in motion might carry on for months, a year in some cases, but there would be no more stimulus. My God, the news tomorrow will be unique in history.

Karl Van Riebeeck, staring at the pillar of smoke, was so caught up in his thoughts that he failed to notice a man parachuting to the ground a mile to his right, nor did he notice a disheveled young man climb out of a haystack, slowly edging behind him from fifty feet away. The sound of a bolt being jerked back snapped him out of his trance and he spun, recognizing the trained face. His hand flew up out of reflex as if to ward off the bullets. He was thinking, the possibility of blind luck always exists and should always be taken. The roar of the gun knocked him back off his feet, dead before he hit the ground.

Moments later the black Mercedes swung out onto the road; it drove through Marquette and turned south toward the French border. After several minutes it passed ambulances traveling in the opposite direction. Jerry watched them recede in the rear-view mirror and smiled to himself. A waste of gas he thought.

Looking at the road sign, he worked a problem in his head, fifteen miles to the border, and fifty to Reims. Sixty-five miles to Reims, he knew of a doctor there, who was discreet for a price. "One hour," he said out loud. Anybody can last for an hour. "Talk about luck," he thought, "talk about luck."

***

On February 2, 1978 a jeep was towed out of the White Volta River, and the remains of its two occupants were placed in caskets for transport via Dougoudou. Henry Renard was buried three days later near Lyon in a simple ceremony attended by several friends.

Connie Carlton was laid to rest in a family plot near Seattle, Washington. The service was observed by most of her family.

In early December, attorneys employed by General Systems of Jersey managed to have charges dropped in a Federal case against their major stockholder. Lack of evidence was stated as a reason for dismissal of the charges.

Jerry and Nicole Carlton found November and late spring to be lovely in Brisbane.

The End

About the Author

Roger C Horton, born 1942, grew up in southern Florida. He was drawn to the water, and sailed the Florida coast, Bahamas in his early teens. He began working offshore on foreign flag, commercial sailing vessels at the age of fifteen, plying mainly the waters of the Caribbean.

As an Army sergeant, he served In Viet Nam, in 1968 and 1969. Discharged in Sept. of 1970, he returned to the US Merchant Marine. Holding an (Unlimited Master of Oceans) license, Captain Horton has made voyages to the world's ports for fifty years, as well as traveling widely when ashore to include trekking across sub-Saharan Africa. A writer of novels, short stories, poetry, he has also been, for decades, a successful Marine Artist and illustrator. It is obvious to those who have read his work that he is a writer with a wide life experience, that creates a totally captivating world of words. For those readers, the ones who want believable human tales on land and sea, and stories of people whose lives are woven into the fabric of our times, Horton's novels will leave them satisfied, long after the last page is turned.